*An **Expanded Edition** of the Soul-Stirring Classic*

BETWEEN
FATHERS AND SONS

An African-American Fable

ERIC V. COPAGE

ISBN: 979-8-9882906-8-1 (Softcover)
ISBN: 979-8-9882906-7-4 (Hardcover)
ISBN: 979-8-9882906-1-2 (eBook)

Cover and interior design/formatting
by Vickie Swisher, Studio 20|20, Toledo, IL

Printed by IngramSpark® in the United States of America

Second printing edition 2024

Black Pearls Living
P.O. Box 1847
125 Glenridge Ave.
Montclair, NJ 07042

www.blackpearlsliving.com

Table of Contents

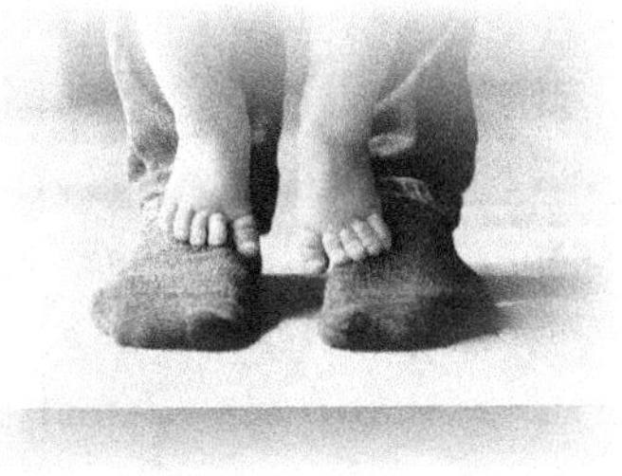

INCANTATION

My name is Miles Johnson. I grew up in Oakwood, a midsized Northeastern suburb a stone's throw from The City. You can see The City's silhouette from some parts of town—the wedges, spires, and arcs of buildings that symbolize networks of enterprise and ambition. Many of my friends' parents prospered there as business owners, lawyers, accountants, and corporate managers. Oakwood neighborhoods that don't enjoy city vistas still offer the cocoon of well-swept streets canopied by the branches of maple, ash, and oak trees. In spring and summer, when the light is just right, reflections from the leaves of those trees give the houses—ranging from modest multifamily dwellings to mansions—a greenish tinge and gently dancing patterns of sunlight and shade.

But I would soon find out in the starkest terms that a boy must struggle to become a man even in my peaceful town—where squirrels dart across quiet streets dappled with shadows. And even in my town, with its strong African-American presence—where proud talk of our black heritage, our great African past, and the symbolic meanings of kente cloth take on an almost magical significance—a black boy needs guidance on his quest to become a black man.

And so it was with me in the year 2000. I was a thirteen-year-old on a hot but mercifully dry Saturday afternoon in early August, sitting on a metal folding chair in the middle of our front lawn. Behind me, the modest, three-story colonial house I shared with my widowed father, my grandmother, and my two siblings, Douglass and Ida, seven-year-old twins.

Headphones covered each of my ears with cushioned black circles the size of Oreo cookies, and a thin black cord snaked down, connecting them to the Walkman cassette player hooked to my belt. The headphones and player were birthday gifts I had received eight months earlier from Dad, and ever since then, the rhythms and rhymes of hip-hop groups like Brand Nubian and Naughty by Nature and rappers like Q-Tip and Nelly had been the heartbeat and lifeblood of nearly every move I made.

Today, although the headphones still covered my ears, the music had stopped, and the rhythmic clapping and the voices of my little sister chanting along with one of her friends seeped in:

> Down, down, baby
> Down, down the roller coaster
> Sweet, sweet, baby
> I'll never let you go

They and Douglass and several of his friends stood at the edge of the lawn near the sidewalk. The girls played their hand game beside a card table draped with a paper tablecloth decorated with a kente-cloth pattern at its border. Taped to the side of the table facing the street was a carefully stenciled sign whose bold black letters read: LEMONADE – 75 Cents. COOKIES – 25 Cents Each. Douglass was behind the table. He had just finished tipping the enormous cylindrical cooler, so the final drops of lemonade trickled from the spout into a paper cup. He had picked up the cup and extended it to the last customer, a tall, middle-aged woman made even taller by the Rollerblades she wore. Dark-skinned with a medium-length, platinum-colored natural haloing her head, her resting facial expression resembled Maya Angelou's look of serene bemusement. She wore cherry-red shorts and a white tank top. In her hand, she held a bill she'd fished out of the blue denim fanny pack decorated with black Adinkra symbols slung just beneath her waist. She received the drink with one hand, and with the other she gave Douglass what he later told me was a five-dollar bill.

I saw her mouth the words, "Keep the change, baby." Then, holding the brimming cup just above her waist, she silently glided away on the sidewalk without spilling a drop of the beverage.

Shimmy, Shimmy cocoa pop
Shimmy, Shimmy pow
Shimmy, Shimmy cocoa pop
Shimmy, Shimmy pow!

I remember being lost in thought and staring in the general direction of my siblings. As recently as a month ago, I had worked the stand with them on the Fourth of July. It was a tradition in our family— selling refreshments in front of our house every Independence Day since I was four or five years old. It was the perfect spot, with the parade passing in front of our house.

After the lemonade sold out (and it sold out every Fourth of July), I, and later the twins and I, counted up to fifty dollars in profit—a king's ransom for a child at that time, even splitting the money three ways. We would open the stand on occasion throughout the summer, even though the reduced foot traffic on our street meant business was far from brisk without a parade.

But I had turned thirteen the previous December and felt I had outgrown selling lemonade or getting excited about surprise visits to Toys R Us. Working at a lemonade stand now seemed childish. So, at the end of this past Fourth of July, I decided I would leave it to my little brother and sister alone.

As I watched them chatting with their friends, my mind started to wander over the prospects for the coming school year. I would be starting a new school, high school, and as a ninth grader, I knew I would be on the school's lowest rung. Don't get me wrong—I was proud of graduating and moving on to high school, but I also anticipated my loss of status, which counted for a lot. I know that now, but I had an even keener sense of it then. I felt as if I was being sent back to the end of a long line.

"Miles! Miles!" My attention snapped away from my reveries, and my head swiveled in the direction of the demanding voice. It was Dad, who was standing on our front porch about twenty feet behind me. Forty-three years old at the time, his lean, muscular frame testified to his health-conscious diet and years of self-defense training. His skin was the color of a brand-new penny, and his squarish face and short-cropped black hair made many people mistake him for the dad in the television sitcom *Moesha.*

"*Miles!*" Dad called out again, with slightly more aggravation in his voice.

I pushed the headphones down so the earcups hugged my collarbone. The outside world flooded in.

"Go help your brother and sister pack up, Son," he continued. "I need all of you to lend a hand with dinner."

I rose from my perch and walked over to Ida and Douglass as they said goodbye to their friends.

Douglass was a linguistic trapeze artist, swooping, swinging, and diving among puns, alliterations, rhymes, and other kinds of wordplay with precocious ease. Douglass, always advanced when it came to English, had begun playing with foreign languages about a year earlier, during his daily phone conversations with Dad, who had been on a two-week-long business trip in Europe. He used a different language for saying goodbye to each of his friends: *adios, au revoir, ciao, auf wiedersehen.* Ida said goodbye to her friend in her usual quiet voice. The rest of the family and I constantly reminded Ida to speak up, but she still spoke so reticently you'd think she was a member of Michael Jackson's soft-spoken clan.

By the time I reached the twins, they had started to make a mess of dismantling the lemonade stand. My sister had put the lid on the shoebox full of the day's earnings and was trying to carefully peel the sign from the table. My brother staggered toward the house, awkwardly holding the plastic bag filled with the remaining paper cups with one hand while embracing the empty ten-gallon cooler by gripping its two handles with both. The container alone would have been difficult to carry for someone his size.

"Need any help, Douglass?" I asked.

"No, thanks," said Douglass, who had put down his cargo and was rubbing the pain from his hands.

"Be careful," I cautioned him. "You don't want to hurt yourself."

I quickly freed the handmade sign and gave it to Ida to carry along with the shoebox. Then I folded up the table, grabbed it by one edge with one hand, and lumbered back to the house, seizing the metal chair by the back with my other hand along the way.

As I walked to the back door of our house, my attention began drifting again, this time to Dad's expectations of me. Throughout my life, Dad had emphasized excellence. He did so less through lectures than with a couple of well-chosen words and very firm action: bad test—no sports that weekend; teacher reports inattentiveness in class—no television. That may sound tough, perhaps too exacting and unforgiving. And I didn't appreciate it at the time. But looking back on it as an adult, I think I was blessed.

I remember long before any conversations about having high standards, my father began suggesting behaviors that would "assure progress even in an unfair world," as he liked to say. For instance, he often recommended I "eat the frog first," which meant to attack the unpleasant parts of a task before moving on to the rest. "Before you start anything," he'd say, "scan it for the most difficult parts" and "go over your work after it's finished." Dad would make suggestions like these time and time again and encourage me to memorize them—or as he put it, take "skull notes"—of his recommendations and review them before doing homework assignments, practicing piano, or starting any other activity.

If I were going through a rough patch when it came to academics, Dad would work patiently with me, guiding me through the lesson, calmly helping me look at a problem first this way, then that way, then another way to help me find the answer for myself.

My bookshelf groaned under the weight of soccer, T-ball, softball, and basketball trophies I had earned since kindergarten, playing in the town's various leagues. Granted, some of them were participation trophies, but I never returned home from a game with a clean uniform. My involvement in the town leagues and traveling teams was due not only to my physical ability—Dad would not have let me join any extracurricular sports if I hadn't kept up with my grades.

But Dad wasn't only a stern taskmaster; he supported me no matter what at sports events. When my team won or when I performed particularly well, he gave me enthusiastic high-fives; at a loss, a discreet hug or a rub on the shoulder. I half resented what I thought was "babying," but looking back, I'm grateful for his vote of acceptance and confidence that said, "you'll always be a winner to me."

Since my thirteenth birthday, however, there had been a sea change in the emotional climate of our household. Storm clouds of doubt gathered over what had been the light and warmth of my father's encouragement. Razor-toothed flashes of impatience were followed by the crack and rumble of oppressive "lessons." Just before school let out for summer vacation, he talked to me yet again about the importance of black achievement. I had had enough of him shoving his anxiety down my throat and I pushed back. "Why do we always have to explain ourselves to other people? Why do we always have to be well-behaved and always be at our best? It's exhausting!"

Anger flared from his eyes, and I involuntarily flinched, fearing he was going to haul off and hit me, although he had never struck me before. But he took a deep breath. And then another.

"This is not about other people," he said deliberately. "And sometimes the only sensible thing to do is to misbehave, to break rules created solely to hold you back." He was about to say something else but stopped short as if an unexpected thought had popped into his head. "Why would you look for an excuse to do anything other than your best?" he asked, puzzled.

"Dad," I replied, exasperated, "I just want to be left alone. I just want to be myself without expectations, explanations, or apologies!"

He thought for a long moment, furrowed his brow, and finally responded with the concentration of a software engineer debugging a code so that a program works properly.

"Listen, Son," he began, "I'll ask you this: when you start a basketball game, do you go in hoping it will end with a tie or even with your team losing?"

Trick question. I wanted to roll my eyes at its absurdity. But I didn't dare do that—Dad was clearly not in the mood for any kind of "lip."

"I guarantee you," he continued, when I withheld my response, "the other team, even if you know some of them as friends, have come ready and willing to beat you. Whether they can is up to you. People will grin ear to ear and tell you it's

OK to aspire to be just OK. They are neither your friends nor your allies. They are enemies rooting for you to lose."

I longed for a return to the casual and easy conversations Dad and I used to have. I loathed what was happening now—talks that almost always deteriorated into harangues mostly centering around the words "black man." Dad would repeat those words in these lectures. It was as if he believed he could conjure this "black man" out of me by repeating those words often enough, yet he never explained to me exactly what a "black man" is. And for reasons that elude me to this day, I felt embarrassed to ask him.

I first remembered hearing that pair of words at the beginning of the year, shortly after my birthday. It was a snowy day, and Dad and I were buying the Sunday newspaper from Blackmun, whose full name was Charles A. Blackmun, the owner of a corner convenience store in town. Our family had known Blackmun since we first moved to Oakwood a decade earlier, and he and my father had become friendly, if not friends. But Dad always made a point of praising Blackmun's entrepreneurial spirit and attention to detail to me.

Blackmun was coming up the basement stairs located in an alcove a few feet behind the counter when I made a comment to my father—I don't remember what exactly—but the response it elicited from Dad and Blackmun remains vivid in my memory. The two men beamed.

Looking at my father and pointing an approving thumb in my direction, Blackmun said, "Spoken like a black man."

"Like a *true* black man," Dad added proudly.

I was confused by their comments—and somewhat taken aback. What did being black have to do with anything?

As I entered the mudroom through the back door of our house on this August day, I leaned the table and chair against a wall and continued into the kitchen. The dreamy tones of a vibraphone—Bobby Hutcherson's rendition of "Maiden Voyage"—floated from the radio sitting on the countertop underneath the kitchen cabinets. With each tap of a mallet on the instrument's metal bars, a brief, glittering plume of sound seemed to appear in midair. A mouthwatering aroma filled the room; Dad was steaming up the place, making jambalaya for dinner. Ida and Douglass raced in and began to bang around as they made trips to the cupboard and drawers under the countertop for plates, silverware, and glasses to set the picnic table in our backyard. I spread out a dish towel near the sink, turned on the faucet, and put my hand under the streaming column of water until it ran cold. I then began to pull the leaves from the head of iceberg lettuce for the salad. I washed, shredded, and dried the leaves, then put them in the teakwood salad bowl. Dad noticed I had not pulled all the leaves from the head and some of those in the bowl were still quite damp.

"Son, I'd like you to pull *all* the leaves off the head of lettuce, then dry them *completely*," he said firmly. "Now, take it back and do it again."

I dumped the leaves in the bowl on the dish towel with a violent shake, then started ripping the remaining leaves from the head. What's the big deal, I wondered to myself. A little water wouldn't hurt anybody. Besides, the salad was going to be wet with dressing eventually. But I didn't raise those points with Dad. I knew that I'd risk getting another one of those lectures. And over the past nine months, I had already received enough to last a lifetime—maybe two or three lifetimes.

As I pounded the leaves dry, I heard Dad ask, "Are you about through with that lettuce?"

"Mm-hmm," I grunted barely audibly, hoping that minimal response would keep him at bay.

"Miles, I asked you a question."

Mercifully, just then, I heard the familiar crunching sound of car tires rolling over our gravel driveway. Dad's mother was returning from her weeklong trip to Oak Bluffs, a town on the island of Martha's Vineyard in Massachusetts.

"Grandma's home," sang out Douglass, who had finished setting everything on the table. Perhaps I had been given a reprieve. A few minutes later, Grandma stepped through the back door. She was a trim woman of medium height. She looked stylish, as always, today wearing her favorite dress—a white Tracy Reese–designed sleeveless sundress in a red floral print, which Grandma had made herself from a dress pattern. It complemented her cappuccino-colored skin with its spray of freckles, concentrated primarily on her face. Smiling broadly, she was about to speak, probably about her adventures with her Delta sorority sisters during her time away, but the moment her eyes alighted on the twins, she bent down, opened her arms wide, and exclaimed joyfully, "Give Grandma some sugar!" as they rushed and playfully tackled her in their eagerness for a hug and a kiss.

Although Grandma was sixty-five years old, there was a timeless effervescence about her. Looking back, I think part of her lively appearance came from her eyes. I had noticed with most people around her age, their eyes seemed to go dull as if clouded over with cataracts and fatigue. Grandma's eyes had an alertness and clarity that reminded me of my siblings' eyes. She looked at the world avidly. It seemed you could see her pupils dilate as she looked around as if she were attempting through a gentle force of will to ingest all the things and sensations of life, so they became a part of her. I never knew Grandma's husband, my grandfather—he died before I was born. Although she dated and had lots of friends and otherwise kept occupied with volunteer work at a local hospital, she focused her energies on being the female figure in the household and helping Dad raise us.

"Something sure smells *gooooooood!*" Grandma said melodiously. She approached the kitchen cart Dad had wheeled near the stove where he had been fixing dinner. The top of the cart was neatly arrayed with stainless steel measuring spoons and Pyrex measuring cups.

"You just won't give up using these things, will you, Son," Grandma said, shaking her head in feigned exasperation. She picked up a measuring spoon and gave it a comically thorough inspection—pretending to check its depth, flexibility, weight—tapping it on the cart then putting it next to her ear and periodically nodding as if listening to its whispered cooking tips. When she noticed Dad was too busy rummaging around for something in the back of the refrigerator to appreciate her antics, she stealthily turned her attention to the jambalaya simmering in a covered cast-iron Dutch oven on the stovetop. Like a culinary ninja, Grandma, in one silent swoop, grabbed the oven mitt hanging from a magnetized hook on the oven door, lifted the hot lid off the pot with it, and quietly laid the cover on an unused burner. So far, so good. Peeking over her shoulder to make sure Dad was still preoccupied, she picked up the wooden spoon lying next to the burner and dipped it into the pot. She put a dollop of the stew on the back of her hand, tasted it, and frowned. A row of half a dozen small stainless steel bowls, each filled with a different spice, sat on the portable cart next to the measuring cups. Grandma grabbed the bowl containing ground cayenne pepper and stirred two large pinches of it into the pot. When she tasted the stew this time, she smiled, then swiftly returned the bowl to the cart. A nanosecond later, Dad shut the refrigerator door, turned around, and moved towards the stove. Grandma gave him a wide "cat that ate the canary" grin. When Dad stopped, seemingly confused by her expression, she flashed him a peace sign with fingers tinged with the incriminating red dust from the pepper. Now it was Dad's turn to shake his head in feigned exasperation.

Grandma had been living with us since my mother's death from a brain tumor shortly after the twins' birth. Mom had always placed flowers strategically around our house to make it a home. Or she'd decorate our mantel with a simple, colorful piece of fabric to cheer up the place. Even when Dad was struggling to get his public relations business on its feet, and there wasn't a dime to spare, Mom had found a way to brighten everything around us. At least, that is what relatives later told me. Regardless, I know now that Grandma added a spot or two of radiance to our home—a seasonally appropriate wreath on the front door, wind chimes on the back porch, large woven baskets lined with cotton sacks for our dirty laundry instead of plain plastic clothes hampers.

"We've finished setting the table," Ida announced to our father after Dad turned his attention back to the stove. "May we watch TV?"

"First, I'd like you both to finish those arithmetic problems I gave you. There are only five of them."

"But, Dad," Douglass whined, "a show on *Africa* is about to come on!"

"The most *African* thing you can do right now is to deal with those problems," Dad said. "Then, if there's time, you can watch whatever you want until dinner is on the table."

Grandma looked at me quizzically for what seemed like a long time before whispering, "Looks like your father has been giving you a hard time again."

"I wouldn't call it a hard time, Mom," Dad said, interrupting Grandma's comment, his full attention suddenly focused on us. Abruptly concentrating on me alone, he continued, "Look, Miles, you're at an age where I don't need to sugarcoat the truth for you. Life can be good, yes, and it can be wondrous. But life is also full of struggles; it is also full of obstacles. Embrace both the wondrous and the struggles with discipline and joy. When I was your age, my father told me something I'll never forget ..."

And on and on and on—a barrage of words rat-a-tatting towards me like machine-gun fire and so predictable over the past few months I practically had them memorized. I could even quote the next lines, which ran through my head before they had left Dad's mouth: *Everybody chooses from a toolbox of attitudes and actions when dealing with the difficulties of life. Your choice of tools determines the distinction and effectiveness with which you meet your trials. You can choose ignorance, indolence, and pessimism—or intelligence, diligence, and hope ...*

What puzzled me was why Dad was wearing out his words of wisdom and why now? There was also a good portion of worry in his voice when he launched into this subject. I resented the worry more than the words themselves. I had always done well in school—I was in the accelerated math class in junior high, for Christ's sake! But Dad's nagging seemed like he was contradicting what he had been telling me all my life until then. I felt he was suddenly saying, *I don't believe in you!*

A couple of hours later, the jambalaya and Grandma's secret recipe sweet potato pie were just tasty memories, and it was time for the twins to get ready for bed. As usual, they went up to the second-floor bathroom they shared with me. Downstairs in the living room, I could hear the water running as they brushed their teeth and washed up. Typically, they would run the few steps to their bedroom and put on their pajamas—Ida's favorite had images from Disney's *The Lion King*; Douglass favored his Power Rangers sleepwear. Douglass would then scamper to the second-floor landing and announce, "We're ready, Daddy!" Dad would walk up the stairs and read them a chapter from one of the Harry Potter novels, Julius Lester's version of the Uncle Remus stories, or tales based on the Arabian Nights. But their favorite story, and mine too in the days when Dad tucked me into bed, was a story he made up. It was about protagonists around our age outfoxing a wide range of foes while riding their "Night Mare"—a horse Dad described as "the color of a moonless sky" decked out in colorful enchanted quilts that served as armor.

~

That night, not long after Dad had gone to their room, I made my way to my bedroom, which was across the hall from the twins' room. When I reached the landing, I heard Dad capping off the evening ritual by reciting Ida and Douglass's special prayers, the way he had once said them to me:

"Dear God," Dad said in a firm, resonant voice. "Thank you for giving my daughter, Ida, and my son, Douglass, strong, healthy minds and strong, healthy bodies. Thank you for making them successful in everything they do. Amen."

Then he gently ended with the coda, "I'll see you in your dreams, my chocolate prince and princess. And you'll be in my dreams. I love you both very much. Ni-night."

I'd been in my room for about thirty minutes listening, as usual, to music on my headphones when I thought I heard a commotion in the house. The music was so loud, though, I wasn't sure. I pulled my headphones down from my ears, and the full-bodied bass from Missy Elliott's "The Rain (Supa Dupa Fly)," became a tinny vibration against the front of my neck. I pushed the Walkman's off button and, in the ensuing silence, made my way downstairs to the living room where the twins soon joined me. The three of us were astonished at what we saw. The room looked as if a wrecking crew had passed through. A chair lay on its side; the marble-topped coffee table was askew because one of its legs had been broken. A ceramic vase cherished by my mother lay cracked on the floor; the arrangement of hydrangea, roses, and jasmine it had held splayed halfway out of the vase in a puddle of water. Grandma was sitting cross-legged on the floor quietly sobbing, cradling Dad's head in her lap. Dad's lips were slightly parted, his breathing shallow, his complexion waxen.

"Your father passed out," Grandma said. In the panic beginning to envelop me, I heard the piercing caterwauling of an ambulance. "I'm going with him to the hospital," Grandma continued. "I'll call you as soon as we get there."

I ran to open our front door just as the ambulance rolled up in front of our house. Two EMTs jumped out of the cab and walked briskly to the back of their vehicle. They flung open the back doors, pulled the gurney out, and snapped the legs into place. The black polyurethane wheels made a muted clickety-clack sound as the paramedics rushed the gurney over our concrete walkway, up the wooden porch steps, through our foyer, and into the living room, where Dad and Grandma were. The paramedics pitched quick questions to Grandma about Dad's condition and lifted him onto the gurney, where they ran an IV line into his arm and put an oxygen mask over his face. I caught a glimpse of something I'd never thought I'd see in Dad's face: fear.

In a blur, the paramedics whisked the gurney through the house and out the front door. Grandma, the twins, and I followed.

"Pray for your father," Grandma said to Ida, Douglass, and me once we were outside. The twins and I remained standing in front of the house while

Grandma hurried to catch up with the EMTs heading back to their ambulance.

As Grandma approached the gurney, my soul inexplicably divided: part of me gazed at my siblings and me against the backdrop of our house as we looked on in stunned helplessness at the scene unfolding in front of us. Simultaneously, part of me floated just above Grandma's right shoulder as she bent over Dad, speaking to him constantly, reassuringly—low and fast—as they made their way along our walkway and into the ambulance. Her patter reminded me of the sound of water coursing over rocks, but it was the reverberation of Grandma's voice, repeating something over and over and over again, a torrent of words—an incantation.

I tried to understand what Grandma was saying but could seize upon only one thing, one word that repeatedly punctuated the river of sound streaming over her lips. After the strobing red-and-white lights of the ambulance were swallowed up by the semidarkness provided by our suburban streetlamps and the arrhythmic yelping of the siren faded into a spooky silence, I ushered the twins into the house, but the resonance of one word, the word Grandma had repeated continuously, like a chant, lingered in my ears.

Hours after the ambulance had left, the word's ghostly reiterations remained. I opened the front door and returned outside into the warmth of the night, and silently mouthed the word to myself.

And the word I mouthed was *Love*.

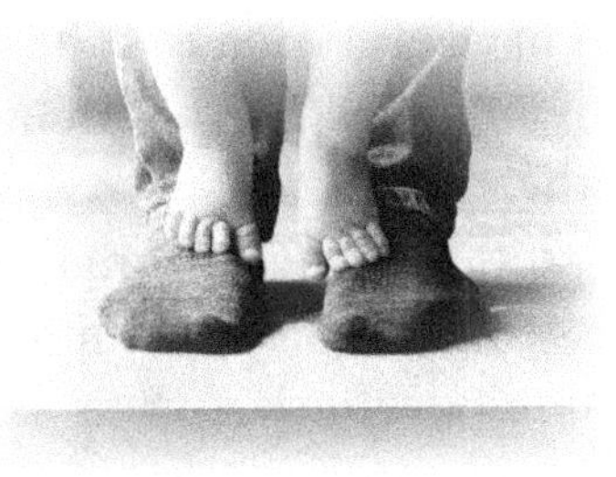

THE
KENTE
CLOTH

I couldn't remember the last time I had cried. As a six-year-old, I didn't know what had hit me when Mom passed away. Dad explained it by saying Mommy loved me and my brother and sister very much, but God had called her back. God had called her home. Mommy was happy, Dad had said. She was a brown angel. She was one of the twinkling stars at night. I had no tears back then, just confusion. Why had God called her back? Why had He taken her away from me and my infant brother and sister?

But now, stationed before Dad's open grave on this hot, overcast day in late August—the air a damp attack to my forehead, my armpits, the nape of my neck, my back—I felt my knees buckling from the numbness of grief; I tried to stifle the great sobs erupting from my chest as I watched the casket lowered into the ground.

When we all turned away from the grave, heading to our cars to go home, the mourners huddled around our family, offering their condolences. I stood next to my grandmother, who wrapped her arms around Ida and Douglass, standing side by side in front of her. I felt the warmth of my grandmother's shoulder against mine and an increasing press of flesh and souls of our relatives, Dad's friends, Grandma's friends, my sister's and brother's friends and their parents, my friends and their parents, and teachers and neighbors. Yet, though friends and family embraced me on all sides, I felt alone. I felt as if I had crossed some boundary or, more accurately, had been pushed blindfolded and falling into a perilous frontier of the unknown.

Suddenly, a pair of hands—fingers heavy with gold rings engraved with images of a spiderweb, four-headed crocodiles, and an abstract filigreed pattern—clasped my hand and guided me out of the crowd trying to comfort me. I instantly recognized those hands; they had given me change for many a candy bar, ice cream sandwich, and cupcake ever since I was in elementary school.

"I was devastated to hear about your father," said Blackmun, the convenience store owner in our neighborhood. No one knew for sure how old Blackmun was. Because his trim mustache and goatee were generously flecked with gray, as was the receding tide of close-cropped hair on his head, some people guessed he was in his early fifties. Yet he had the body build of a much younger man, and he usually carried himself with vitality and agility. At times, however, he seemed frail and infinitely old, his mental clarity questionable and subject to "spells." There were even those in town who referred to him—well out of his earshot—as "that crazy brotha, Blackmun," an eccentric but harmless "old fool."

Blackmun himself was mum on the personal details of his life. What was truly odd about him, and what I remember most, was the uncanny feeling I and many others often got when he talked about black history—how the African queen Nzinga outsmarted a Portuguese official, or the bloody Nat Turner slave rebellion, for instance. Blackmun's accounts were vivid and full of minute detail—how enslaved Africans sought a place close to the cotton field to urinate during up to fifteen hours working on blazing humid days, the acrid smell of blood as a whip lacerated human flesh to the bone, the forbidding patches of darkness shifting in the moonlit forest while traveling on foot towards a stop on the Underground Railroad. It was as if Blackmun recalled them from firsthand experience—from memory—rather than from something he had read in a book.

Today, at the funeral and burial, Blackmun wasn't wearing one of his many dashikis, but rather the regulation funeral attire of a dark suit, white shirt, and dark tie. A kente cloth stole draped his shoulders, however.

Blackmun put two comforting hands on my upper arms as I faced him and looked into his eyes. "I admired your father very much. As much as I know he is a loss to you, he is also a loss to the neighborhood. To our town. His passing is a loss to all of us. He told me he had been looking forward to seeing you become a black man," Blackmun added.

A black man, I repeated silently to myself. Those words again! I wished I could figure out what Dad and Blackmun meant. I thought about the black men I'd grown up with, that I'd seen on the streets, in movies, and on television. I thought of the black men I'd read about in newspapers, magazines, and books. I thought of Dad. *Do I have to do anything special to become a black man? I wondered. Does it simply happen when I reach a certain age, I asked myself, and was I about to reach that age? Do I have to walk a certain way or talk a certain way to be a black man? Does it depend on the clothes I wear—a uniform I slip into once I graduate from a particular grade? Or was it simply having experienced a loss or a deep enough pain? Did I become a black man carrying Dad's casket down the church steps? Above all, what is a black man?* Right now, I didn't feel much like any kind of man at all. I felt insignificant, like the fading echo of a very small child.

I looked at Blackmun again and, for the first time, really noticed the kente cloth he was wearing. Blackmun had a wide assortment of kente cloths—all vibrant with reds, greens, blues, golds, and blacks, all woven of the highest quality silk. Every year around the Martin Luther King Jr. holiday, the school superintendent would invite Black-mun to the schools in our town to talk about the meaning of the cloths and the symbols on other African fabric, jewelry, and artifacts. As I pondered the cloth hung around Blackmun's neck, he began to lift the stole over his head and carefully began handing it to me. There was ritualistic deliberateness to his movements as if he was handing over a sacred object. But as I watched the cloth arch over Blackmun's head and down past his face, I noticed the colors of this kente were dull, the fabric dirty, frayed, and moth-eaten. There were even stains from—blood? Grease? Coffee? I couldn't begin to imagine what. Why was he handing me this nasty, raggedy old piece of cloth? Why was he wearing it at my father's funeral?

"I know your father would have wanted you to have this," Blackmun said, holding the kente cloth in front of him, waiting for me to take it. I was baffled and a little repelled by the gesture. From my perspective, it was as if he were offering me a mushy, half-eaten apple. It was a revolting and—well, kind of a crazy thing to do. I reached for the cloth with reluctant hands.

"Take care of it," Blackmun continued, ignoring what surely must have been a look of disgust on my face as I warily drew the cloth towards me as if it might be contaminated. "Keep it near you, always, even if that nearness is only in your heart. Any problems, any problems at all, feel free to call on me. Or, if you just want to talk, stop by. Remember, we're in this together."

When I returned home, I threw the kente cloth over the inside doorknob of my bedroom door and shut it. But that night, after I got into bed and turned out my nightstand lamp, I gazed for a long time at the cloth, trying to figure out why Blackmun had given me this stained and tattered fabric and why Dad would have wanted me to have it. Night dulled the cloth's already faded colors, except where it was illuminated by blades of moonlight slicing through my partially open venetian blinds. The kente cloth rippled ever so slightly in response to the faint breeze coming from my open window. Bits of the material's geometric patterns seemed to begin a barely noticeable dance in the interplay of darkness and light. A soothing rhythm soon enveloped me, and I felt myself drifting off to sleep. And in that sleep, I had a dream.

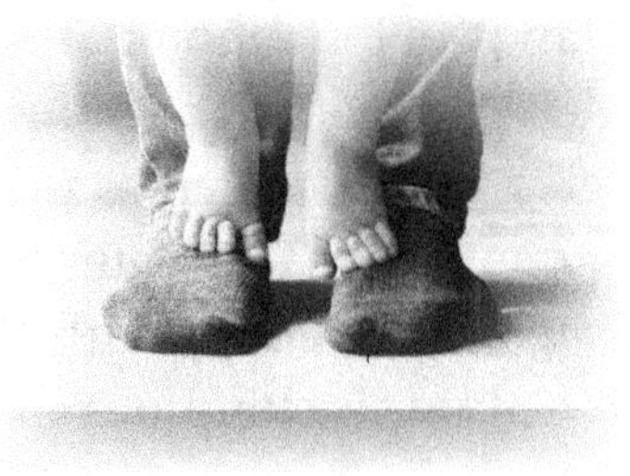

THE
VITAL
QUESTION

The sound of my breathing filled my room, and with every breath, the weight of my body seemed to dissipate into the air. I felt myself expanding beyond the boundaries of my skin. I felt myself rising like an infinitely fine mist, passing through my ceiling, through the clutter in the attic, through the shingles of the roof, and into the humid night air. I continued rising and mingled with the gauzy vapors of the night sky. As I rose, I saw the lights of my neighborhood, the neighborhoods around it, and eventually, The City itself spread out below me before a convergence of clouds covered it. I accelerated as I rose beyond the clouds, zooming through world after world after world after world.

I soared past lands of lofty mountains, rushed over lands of hot desert sands, darted through lands of steaming jungles, and sped across windswept prairies of ice. As I entered each realm, whatever contained my spirit shuddered violently.

I fell with a thud; a cloud of red dust flew up around me. Startled and dazed, I lifted my head and wiped my eyes. It was either sunrise or sunset, I couldn't tell which. I had landed on an endless plain of red-colored sunbaked clay. I scanned the horizonless distance where land and sky merged in the ochre half-light. I squinted and somehow was propelled to a spot half a football field away from a seated man dressed in colorful traditional Ashanti robes. To his right stood another man, also dressed in Ashanti robes. They were situated near a towering baobab tree with its tangle of bare branches. As I rose to my feet, I saw that the seated and standing men were flanked by at least a hundred armed men, distributed evenly on each side.

The armed men, apparently soldiers, stood at attention, each with a rifle resting on his shoulder. I shivered when the two men, their entire retinue of soldiers, and the tree suddenly streaked in my direction as one unit, as if they were atop a single piece of earth. In a heartbeat, they had moved in a herky-jerky, zigzaggy path towards me, and I was dwarfed by the enormity of the tree's gray trunk, its roof of leafless limbs now draping me in a coarse mesh of jagged shadows. The man I presumed to be the king sat on a wooden stool, his legs spread wide, each hand relaxed on its corresponding thigh, a study in authority and equilibrium. He was resplendent in the wedges, spires, and arcs that comprised the jewel-like geometry of the folds of his royal robe. Its colors—ruby red, emerald green, sapphire blue, and glittering gold—were so brilliant they made my eyes ache as if I were looking directly at the sun. I had to turn my head away from their radiance.

Ring upon ring of gold and silver hoops encircled the king's ankles. He wore sumptuous leather flip-flop sandals, their broad black velvet straps decorated with four pinkie finger–sized sculptures in gold of Sankofa, the mythical bird that cranes its long neck backward while holding an egg in its beak, its claws resolutely facing forward. The part of the sandals that touched the king's soles were covered in gold leaf. His feet hovered effortlessly an inch or two above the red earth as if they rested atop the invisible force of another world.

The king's soldiers gazed ahead, expressionless. They wore Union Army uniforms of the American Civil War—light blue pants, gray woolen shirt, dark blue jacket, and a blue cap whose flat crown slouched forward towards its stiff bill on every head. The king looked straight ahead, impassively. He did not seem to notice me. The standing man I took to be the king's adviser. He turned his head in my direction and spoke: "I will tell you a story. When I finish, I will ask you a question. You may not move from that spot until you answer that question. Your life depends on your answer to that question."

With those final words, I heard the clank of metal as the king's soldiers cocked their weapons and pointed them at me.

~

A Black Man guides a half dozen slaves to freedom. At the end of the first day, they make an overnight stop in an empty cabin in a forest. The next morning, when it's time to continue, the former captives refuse to open the cabin door. They are afraid of the wild beasts they heard outside during the night. But the Black Man tells the group he has made dozens of journeys through these parts. He's traveled under daylight, moonlight, and through the moonless darkness. He's slept in cabins, caves, and under the stars in this area. He's traveled in all seasons. He has traveled through rain, sleet, snow, and debilitating heat—through droughts and through floods. He is intimately familiar with the plants and animals in these parts and has even foraged for them and hunted them for food.

I've never seen even one wild beast around here, the Black Man said. The nearest wild beasts are miles away.

We have traveled in forests like this before, said one of the former captives. Despite your reassurances, we know there are wild beasts. We know their signs. We've been mauled by them in broad daylight and bear those scars.

If there are no wild beasts in these forests, another in the group said, what was that ghostly howling all last night?

The wind through trees, the Black Man answered.

What were those shadows moving at the bottom of the door? asked another.

Deer walking towards the nearby pond to drink, the Black Man replied.

What was the scratching outside the cabin's back wall?

Raccoons searching for food, the Black Man responded.

Yet despite every reasonable explanation, the slaves remained steadfast in their belief that wild beasts were right outside the door, ready to devour them, and they refused to budge. Finally, the fugitives confidently followed the Black Man out of the cabin door towards freedom.

~

The king's adviser looked at me solemnly: "How did the Black Man convince the group there were no wild beasts in this forest?"

The sun and stars completed their circuit twenty-one times, and I had no answer to his question. I could smell the stench of adolescent sweat rising from me. My stomach roared with hunger. My throat was raw and parched. The soldiers advanced upon me by one giant step. After another twenty-one circuits of the sun and stars, the soldiers took another step towards me. I was on the edge of despair when I looked up and saw the answer. It streaked far above me like a shooting star across the wine-red sky. I reached for it. I wanted to tell the king's adviser the answer, but no sound escaped when I moved my lips to speak. I looked with pleading eyes while continuing to work my wordless lips. I felt tears of frustration trickle down my cheeks as I struggled to make any kind of sound. The king looked on, unmoved. The soldiers looked on, unmoved. The adviser looked on, unmoved. Finally, I dropped to my knees and tried to scribble the answer with my finger in the bone-hard clay—when I found myself sitting up in my bed, my sheets heavy with sweat, my tongue swollen with thirst, the answer to the vital question gone.

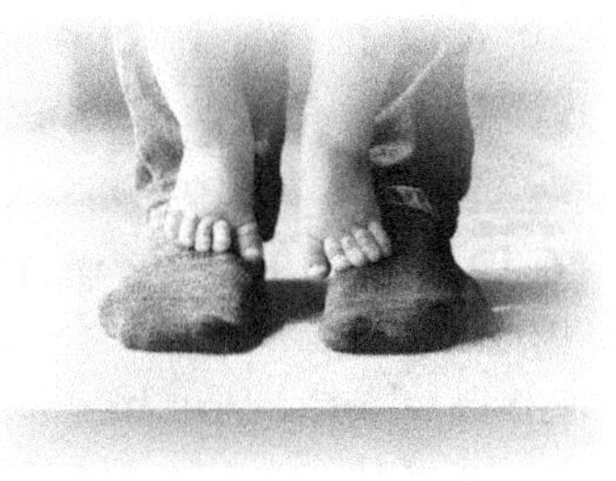

THE
VISIBLE
MEN

I was relieved to start high school a week after the burial. Amid the confusion and grief of the summer's end, I had forgotten most of my worries about my status at school. One of the first new people I got to know was J.J.—Jaxon Jackson.

J.J. was a world traveler even at his tender age. His father, a chemical engineer for different mining companies, had moved the family throughout the country and around the globe every couple of years. J.J.'s parents had divorced three years earlier, and J.J. lived with his mother, a paralegal. She began dating an insurance executive and eventually married him. When J.J.'s stepdad was transferred to the city a year and a half ago, the family moved to Oakwood.

On our first day in high school, the teacher asked us to take down some information in homeroom. When I opened my Trapper Keeper, I noticed I had forgotten to bring pencils or pens. I leaned over to J.J., who sat across the aisle to my left, and asked in a whisper whether he had an extra pencil I could use.

"Sure, no problem," he said, then stood up and called out to the class, "Anybody have a pencil I can borrow?" Half the students raised their hands. J.J. took one from the girl sitting behind him and thanked her.

"Here you go," he said with a generous smile while handing me the pencil, and our friendship was off and running.

J.J. was tall for his age, a beanpole nearing six feet tall, and his voice was deeper than the rest of us in ninth grade, who still squeaked at unexpected moments timed for maximum embarrassment—like when trying to impress a girl with our swagger. J.J.'s voice was not just relatively deep but velvety smooth, like Barry White with a little more treble. He was also a bit ungainly and seemed less to walk than to lope from place to place. You couldn't say he was attractive in any conventional way. Dark circles under his eyes and a discolored front tooth conspired to make him look almost sickly. Perhaps to compensate for his homely appearance, J.J. had developed a distinctive personality that impressed many, including our teachers, as charismatic. He had a feline alertness and playfulness; listening to him during conversations was like watching a cat batting about a mouse, not out of hunger or malice but for sheer amusement.

J.J. was also something of a troublemaker. Word was he had been a "character" throughout his school career. At any rate, in these first few days of high school, he seemed intent on using his formidable personality to provoke attention even more than before. Where our other friends and I were at least a little awed and humbled by our new place in the pecking order, J.J. grabbed the opportunity to make his mark on this clean slate. During the first week of school, our English teacher described a job he had had in Hollywood, working on a movie set. J.J. raised his hand. "Yes, J.J.," the teacher said. "What you're saying is you were a flunky," J.J. quipped. The class tittered as the teacher stammered, "Well, yes, that's essentially correct." There was no hostility in J.J.'s remark, just a simple statement of fact he alone dared voice. But his boldness did not go unnoticed or unadmired.

I liked the way J.J. and his crowd defied the rules; I began to defy those rules with them. I started cutting classes as they did—checking in at homeroom, then leaving school and returning unnoticed during the lunchtime chaos. When I skipped morning classes, I would ride my Cannondale Raven bicycle in one of the town's four large parks, play the latest *NBA Live* video game at one of my new friends' houses, or toss pebbles at buses to see the startled, angry expressions of the passengers. J.J.

always accompanied us on such excursions. Indeed, it was J.J. who seemed to initiate almost everything among our posse.

Once, when J.J. suggested missing a whole day of school, I balked. I had already had a couple of close calls with cops who wondered what we were doing out and about during school hours. (J.J. had too, but he didn't seem to mind.) *What if I should get caught?* I thought. Missing a class or two was on a different scale of misbehavior than getting detention or even being suspended for missing a whole day. *And what if Grandma found out?*

"Aw, man, don't be soft," J.J. said, trying to goad me into coming with him on his daylong adventure. J.J. and I were standing in the hall as school activity swirled around us, students rushing to first period class. With J.J. and I were three of our regular running pals. "What chu trippin' 'bout, dawg?" J.J. continued contemptuously. "You think you gonna get arrested? You scared of going to jail? They don't put you in jail for that!"

"Look," J.J. said, switching tactics, "if cops stop us, they won't do nothin'. They'll just ask for our address and what school we go to. Don't give them the right answers. They don't care."

I was about to defend my position when suddenly J.J. gave me a look that seemed to preclude further discussion. His dismissive sneer made me want to change my mind and go with him. But before I could get my thoughts together and figure out what to say without seeming like a chump, J.J. had turned on his heel. "Peace, I'm out," he said coldly and disappeared down the hall, followed by the other guys.

The loneliness I felt was unlike any loneliness I had ever felt. What made it hurt more was that I felt humiliated. I was sure J.J. and our friends would think of me forever as a coward. But most of all, I felt like a child left with the babysitter while the adults were out having fun.

The next day, first thing after homeroom, I pulled J.J. aside. "Let's go to the mall," I eagerly suggested.

J.J. thought a moment and then shook his head, dismissing the idea.

I persisted with an intensity I myself found disconcerting yet couldn't control. First period was about to start. We had to decide right then if we would escape for the whole day. I enumerated names of stores we could visit, how much fun we could have.

Again, there was, for me, a terrible silence as J.J. mulled over the proposition. "Alright," J.J. drawled and then mentioned a couple of things he'd like to do at the mall. We slipped out of school amid the confusion of changing classes, hopped a bus, and made for the mall.

We went to department stores and tried on oversized Phat Farm jackets popular at the time. Next, to shoe stores to admire the newest Jordan and FUBU kicks. We were thrown out of a sports equipment shop for playing catch with the footballs there. In the preview section of each of the mall's three music stores, we put on earphones and listened to samples of the latest releases from Common, OutKast, and anything produced by The Neptunes. We both mimed performances of the songs, me pretending to work the computer, sampler, and turntable, J.J. doing a precision job of lip-synching.

By early afternoon we got hungry and decided to get something to eat. It was a cool, late September day, and we needed some hot food before stepping back outside. On our way to the fast-food restaurant, I noticed a jewelry store. A thick gold pendant and a bracelet were displayed in the shop's window. "Hey, check that out," I said. "I wonder how much it costs?"

Each of us tried to open the door, but it was locked. A cardboard sign at eye level in the window near the entrance read RING FOR ENTRY. Inside the store, behind the counter, stood a white woman, dressed simply and elegantly in black, a single strand of pearls hung around her neck. She wore her dark hair in a severe bun. Her chic black clothes were young and hip, but the half-glasses she peered over made her look like a priggish old schoolteacher. She was talking with another woman, who wore a large dark overcoat and stood on the counter's opposite side. I figured the woman in the coat was a customer. But when I pushed the buzzer, the woman behind the counter peered over her reading glasses, shook her head, and mouthed to J.J. and me that the store was closed.

J.J. took a concentrated look at the store's RING FOR ENTRY sign, which included other information. "Follow me," he said, and we walked around the corner to a pay phone. He slipped a quarter into the coin slot, and it made a series of musical pings, like miniature chimes, as it dropped. When the dial tone came on, he punched a melody of seven digits.

A muffled woman's voice on the other end of the line: "Hello?"

In his "whitest" voice, J.J. said, "Yes, what are your hours, please?"

A muffled reply.

"So, I can come over right now?" J.J. asked. "OK. Great. I'm heading there. Cheers."

Thirty seconds later, when the saleswoman saw us again at the store's glass door, her expression told us she understood we'd outwitted her. After being buzzed in, I immediately confronted the woman and asked why she had not let us in the first time. But I could tell she wasn't listening to me; she had riveted her attention on J.J., who was wandering along the display cases that ringed the small shop. Ignoring me, she shadowed him from her side of the displays. I quieted down and tried to keep up. J.J. would occasionally stop in front of a case and ask the saleswoman for the price of this item or that, and the woman would give him an icy reply. Then the doorbell rang again. The saleswoman returned to the cash register and buzzed in a mall security guard—a paunchy, balding, upper middle-aged black man of average height. Perhaps he had been some kind of athlete in his younger days, but over the subsequent twenty or thirty years, he had let his body go to pot. His eager seriousness announced he was only too glad to be of service.

The guard nodded to the saleswoman, folded his arms over his chest, and planted himself by the door. He glowered at J.J. and me. I did my best to glower back but noticed out of the corner of my eye that J.J. ignored the man and continued exploring items in the shop, calmly asking for the price of items as they seemed to interest him, apparently unflustered by the saleswoman who remained on his heels.

When J.J. finished, he and I left the store. We wandered around for a couple of minutes, then stopped to figure out the best way to get to the mall's McDonald's. I was about to tell J.J. I couldn't shake the feeling we were being watched when the guard strolled up to us. He had apparently been following us from the time we left the jewelry store. "Are you lost?" he asked unhelpfully.

That was it for me. I let loose with a cataract of curses that was Straight Outta Compton. I tightened my throat to contain the volume of my voice but didn't spare the ferocity. I felt a prickly sensation pass over my skin; the tips of my ears got hot. I leaned towards that idiot as if I was going to knock him out—although I had no intention of doing so. I called him every name in the book, including some I didn't even know I knew. I told him we hadn't stolen anything and defended our right to be there. I never use the N-word, but I flung it at that guard more than once, and not in a brotherly way.

Yet, oddly, I recall thinking during my rant that I felt I *had* done something wrong. In fact, that unwarranted feeling of guilt seemed to fuel my rage.

J.J. waited until I finished, then he answered the guard's questions coolly and succinctly. "No, we ain't lost," he said evenly, "and where we headin' ain't none of yo business, with yo fake-ass badge. Betcha got it from a cereal box. Look," J.J. continued, "you want to call the *real* po-lice, go right on ahead." He then folded his arms over his chest, lowered his head slightly, and stared hard at the guard, a gesture that conveyed defiance rather than menace.

When the guard remained still, J.J. released a couple of disdainful snorts, and the guard stepped back from us, awkwardly turned, and walked away, muttering curses at us under his breath.

But J.J. wasn't finished with him. He waved his right hand demurely in a fake farewell and sang out, "Bye, Felicia," as the guard disappeared around a corner.

I was impressed by how J.J. stood up to the guard as if he had every right to be in that mall. There wasn't a hint of his being intimidated. As I thought about it, my admiration for J.J. deepened.

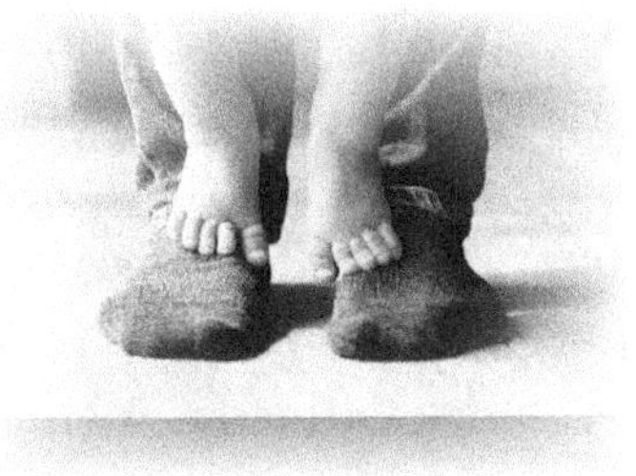

TRUTHS
AND
CONSEQUENCES

On our way home from school, J.J. and I would regularly drop by Blackmun's store to pick up a candy bar or a bag of corn chips. That day, even in the wake of our mall adventure, was no exception. As usual, we hooked up with a couple of our buddies along the way.

For as long as anyone could remember, Blackmun's store had been located at the corner of Walnut and Chestnut, a half block from the trestle over which the commuter trains ran to and from the city. Blackmun's shop had no sign or awning announcing its name. It was just known as the Corner Store, a nondescript brick-and-concrete storefront with a nondescript wood trim painted a nondescript forest green. The store's entrance was located at the corner where the two quiet streets met. Looking at it from outside facing the entrance, one of the store's two windows fanned off to the left along Walnut Street, the other fanned off to the right along Chestnut Street. The window on the busier Walnut Street side was chockablock with advertising signage typical for a small convenience store—cold soda, candy, ice, commuter bus tickets, lottery tickets—but noticeably absent were ads for booze and cigarettes.

The window on the quieter Chestnut Street side provided a view into the store, but Blackmun had constructed a shelf at window level inside where he mounted displays comprised of artifacts relating to black culture and history—a Barbie-style doll of "Julia," the title character of the landmark television show from the late 1960s; goggles worn by Benjamin O. Davis, Jr. when he was a member of the Tuskegee Airmen; a large reproduction of *A Great Day in Harlem*, a photograph of dozens of the biggest of the big dogs of jazz gathered on a brownstone stoop in 1958. Blackmun's modest presentations, which changed every month, included one or two short paragraphs about the object, posed a question, imparted information, or issued a challenge. For instance, Blackmun invited viewers to see how many of the musicians in the picture they could identify in the Harlem photograph.

A similar mix of black history celebration and convenience store congestion greeted customers when they stepped inside the store.

Straight ahead: shelves of toilet paper, laundry detergent, and other household items, along with various single-serving desserts and snack foods crammed the interior's two or three narrow aisles. Beyond them, in a far corner, sat a *Street Fighters II* video arcade game near a refrigerator embedded in a wall; its two large glass doors revealed sodas, sports drinks, teas, and bottled water.

To the immediate right inside the entrance, occupying a couple of shelves under the window facing Chestnut Street stood a pocket-sized library—a rotating selection of books Blackmun would lend out, and samples from his collection of signed photographs of celebrities he had amassed over the years. To the left, on a shelf under that window, were periodicals including black publications.

The glass-topped counter ran from near the refrigerator to a few feet shy of the entrance. Underneath the counter — a colorful riot of packaging for Pop Rocks, Life Savers Holes, Razzles, Hubba Bubbas, and more met the eye and promised a bounty of unnatural flavors designed explicitly by the manufacturers to appeal to the eyes and palates of children and adolescents.

J.J., our friends, and I entered the store—the bell that would have announced our presence had fallen off years ago, and Blackmun had not seen the need to fix it. Blackmun emerged from behind the counter from stairs that led to his basement. He scanned the room, ignoring us, and found what he was looking for on the far end of the counter, near the refrigerator—a kid who looked like he was not much older than my siblings. "For three A's, it will be three dollars," Blackmun said to the child, whose mother stood nearby. Blackmun continued explaining the possible rewards children could receive from him depending on the grades on their tests and report cards. "But a dollar for an A is nothing compared to what you'll get later in life if you study hard and study smart," he said as he counted out three one-dollar bills. It was a line every school-age child in the neighborhood knew by heart, for they were obliged to listen to it if they wanted their prize.

Some parents took a cynical view of Blackmun's offer, saying derisively, "That Blackmun, I bet he gets his dollar back, and more." Others objected to the idea of rewarding their children for something they should do just on principle. Still, for the most part, the adults made a point of dropping by on their way to or from the train station, buying their kitchen matches, juice, and sodas at Blackmun's store, or on Sundays purchasing the paper there, even though for many the local supermarket was more convenient.

When the boy and his mother left the store, Blackmun turned his attention to me, and I walked to where he was standing, where my favorite candy happened to be located. (By now, J.J. and our friends had immersed their attention in the photographs on the shelf.)

"My man, watcha readin'?" Blackmun asked me, using his trademark greeting adopted by what seemed like half of Oakwood.

While fishing in my pocket for money to buy some candy, I shrugged and mumbled, "Knowledge," in standard response to Blackmun's query.

"I saw the twins at the skating rink yesterday," Blackmun continued. "I've never seen two kids have such a good time falling. They had everyone laughing, trying to avoid them. They're getting so big! It seems like just the other day your grandmother was showing me pictures of them getting baptized."

I saw that Blackmun, out of the corner of his eye, noticed J.J. and our friends. They were pointing at different photographs on the shelf underneath the window and laughing like hyenas. "What will it be today, Miles?" Blackmun asked.

"Just these," I said, grabbing four Jolly Rancher lollipops from their container on top of the counter, then handing him the money.

Blackmun was about to give me my change when we heard something crash inside the store. One of Blackmun's framed photos of black artists had plummeted to the floor, face-up, but the glass had shattered completely. It was a glossy 8x10, black-and-white photo of Jimi Hendrix, standing alone onstage, playing a white Stratocaster guitar. Beneath the photo, in the same frame, was a white paper cocktail napkin on which Hendrix had written "Stay Groovy" and autographed. I remembered Blackmun once telling me it was one of his most cherished pieces of memorabilia.

Our friends shuffled their feet and looked embarrassed. They avoided Blackmun's eyes, and through subtle body language—a glance, a barely noticeable tilt of the head—indicated it was J.J. who had dropped the frame. But J.J. stood firm and returned Blackmun's gaze. He was unbowed. He looked Blackmun in the eye for what seemed like a long while. Finally, J.J. said, "Yo, sorry," shrugged, and turned as if to leave the store.

"Pick it up, Son," said Blackmun, the sound of clattering wheels growing louder as a train approached the nearby trestle.

The frosty edge to Blackmun's voice seemed menacing. I'd never heard Blackmun speak to anyone like that before. I sensed a palpable tension in the air. Blackmun and J.J. stared at each other. While I had never seen J.J. fight, he had bragged about his toughness and about "having served" a few guys in previous neighborhoods in which he'd lived. (But only when he *had* to, he always added, smiling.) Oakwood was not the kind of place where J.J. would have to make good on his boasts. Still, J.J. didn't seem the type to talk smack unless he could back it up, so the other guys at school and I took him at his word. And the confrontation I had witnessed a few hours earlier with the mall security guard was added reason to do so.

Blackmun never talked about fights he may have had growing up or as an adult. When discussing boxing matches he had seen, he would focus on the wit and intelligence of the movements and the cast-iron will it takes to withstand brutal, potentially lethal blows. He laughed when talking about World Wrestling Federation stars like The Rock, The Undertaker, or Stone Cold Steve Austin, but noted with approval their resilience and athleticism, even if the violence was cartoonish. But there were rumors in our neighborhood that Blackmun had been a member of a special forces unit—whether in Viet Nam was unclear. Others whispered that Blackmun had once been a member of a street gang ominously called the Jolly Stompers. Dad had mentioned to me more than once, without elaborating, that Blackmun had "come up hard, real hard."

As J.J. and Blackmun faced off, I thought J.J. had the advantage of youth, but Blackmun is bigger, if only slightly. And who knows what moves he might have learned from the military. Although I couldn't imagine Blackmun coming to blows with a thirteen-year-old, even one tall for his age, I nonetheless girded myself to jump between them to stop a brawl.

Then something strange happened ...

Time

Seemed

To

Stop

...Not suddenly like someone flipping a switch, but a slow, steady diminution of sound and motion as if spectral fingers on a dial gradually, very gradually reduced the speed of reality until life was suspended motionless before my senses. In that expanding moment, the crescendo of an approaching train grew slower and deeper until all that remained of the noise of clattering wheels was a low, barely audible hum. A tan plastic shopping bag kicked up by a gust of wind just outside the shop stuttered while soaring through the air, then stopped altogether, as if caught in midflight in a snapshot. A ladybug wandering about on the store's glass countertop became more and more sluggish in its loopy tracks until it ceased to move at all.

I looked in J.J's direction and was startled to see that he and our crew were as motionless as stone statues, locked in mid-gesture and mid-sentence. As I somehow zoomed in on J.J., however, I saw that the irises of his eyes darted around erratically, like the rapid micro-movements of a blind man's eyes behind a pair of sunglasses. Then an unexpected warmth came over me, enveloped me, comforted me as it pulsated through me. It moved with the persistence and effortlessness of ripples caused by a breeze moving over a body of water. I shifted my attention to Blackmun, from whom the warmth seemed to emanate. What I saw was both alien and familiar, terrifying and soothing, ancient and imminent. Blackmun's face—or what I took to be his face, or at least where his face should have been—was an expanding mass of cloudy darkness, like black ink swirling in clear liquid. Where his eyes would have been shone two steely shafts of amber light that by turns cut towards me, then J.J., then to our friends, then back to me, over and over and over, as Blackmun's entire body transformed into a stormy concentration of shadows. The spectacle transfixed me, for I don't know how long until something searing shot up like a solar flare from my tailbone to the base of my skull and radiated out like a supernova throughout the rest of my body. But I wasn't in pain. I wasn't afraid. And I was serene as I observed an explosion erupt with otherworldly silence from the center of Blackmun's roiling silhouette, instantly saturating the store with a boundless blue-white flash that drained all color and eventually all substance from our surroundings, blanketing us finally in a heaving disembodied brilliance.

And then it was over.

Color, substance, sound, and motion returned to life. The low hum became faster and higher until it was again the recognizable clattering of train wheels. The bag landed on the sidewalk, scooted along by the breeze for a few feet, and then rose with another gust of wind. The ladybug continued its loopy journey, then spread its wings and flew away. J.J. blinked a few times and shook his head slightly as if awakening from a trance. Once he was again in the moment, he spoke—his defiance curtailed, but by no means absent. "Sure," he said after a beat, before complying with Blackmun's demand. He picked up the broken frame from the floor. He started to toss it insolently on the nearby counter but caught himself mid-movement and placed it there, in what I took to be an involuntary sign of respect for whatever whammy Blackmun had just laid on us.

As J.J. and our crew turned to leave the store, I heard the guys snickering and saw them slapping J.J. on the back, saying in an audible whisper, "You *owned* him, dawg." But J.J., who still seemed somewhat wobbly, received their admiration with uncharacteristic silence. I noticed he quickly and discreetly raised his thumb to his upper lip and wiped away the trickle of blood that ran from one of his nostrils.

As I began to regain my composure, I automatically turned to follow them out, when Blackmun, holding something in his left hand, called to me. "Miles, you forgot your change." When I reached for it, Blackmun grabbed my forearm with his other hand and held me in its viselike grip. "If you run with people like that, be careful of what you do. You and you alone will be held accountable for your actions. Choose wisely."

I jerked away with all my might from Blackmun's grasp. "I know what I'm doing," I snapped.

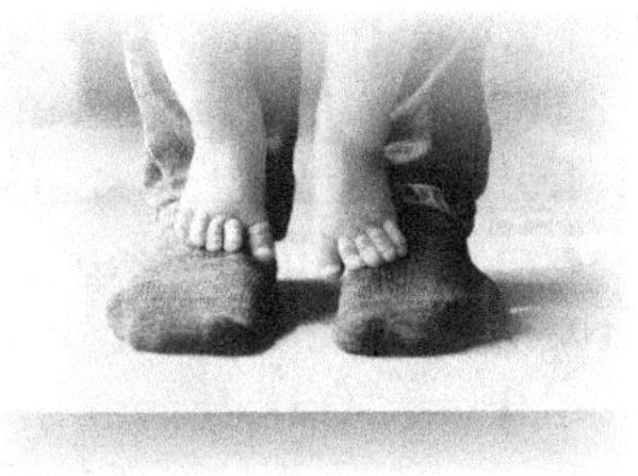

CROSSROADS

An autumnal crispness sheared the early November air. Rich shadows and the deep golden light of sunrise laid their long fingers across the town. The remaining leaves on Oakwood's trees trembled, flew off their branches, and, once fallen, formed a carpet of red, gold, brown, and yellow that rustled and rippled in the wind.

It had been six weeks since my first trip to the mall with J.J. During those six weeks, we had managed to become the two most popular guys in school, or at least in our grade. Admirers and hangers-on crowded our lunch table, and we were on everyone's party invitation lists. Just when the fall party season had kicked into high gear, Grandma told me that she had found temporary work in the hospital where she had been volunteering. Since Dad's estate wouldn't be settled until sometime in the new year, we could use the money.

"Miles, I'm going to have to work afternoons and evenings, Tuesday through Saturday, so you'll have to come straight home after school," Grandma announced one morning in the kitchen while fussing over the twins as she rushed to prepare them for their school bus. "Unfortunately, that means your Friday and Saturday nights will be spoken for, also."

My heart sank. It's not that this was unexpected. I knew Grandma had been planning to get a job. And I knew that would mean I'd have additional responsibilities. But I hadn't figured my new duties would annihilate my social life.

She pulled a paper napkin from its holder on the kitchen table, walked to the sink, and dampened two corners of the napkin in water streaming from the faucet. "You've babysat for the twins plenty of times before, so I know you can handle it," Grandma said, as she cleaned the corner of one of Ida's eyes with one wet part of the napkin and used the other corner to wipe Douglass's mouth. Checking the twins' Mutant Ninja Turtle backpacks for their lunch and field trip permission slips, she added, "Besides, they're practically old enough now to take care of themselves."

I knew Grandma had no other choice, yet I still felt put-upon. I had finally become a big deal at school, and now, just as parties were getting underway, I would have to babysit for the twins every single night.

One Saturday morning, a week after Grandma had started her new job, I was walking around the neighborhood, letting off steam, when I found myself standing outside Blackmun's store. It was the first time I'd been there in quite a while. Under J.J.'s influence, I had avoided Blackmun after the photograph incident. "Who needs that crazy jerk telling me what to do?" J.J. had snapped. I was about to move on when I heard Blackmun call out to me.

"Whatcha readin', fam?" asked Blackmun, who was wearing a Hampton University sweatshirt. He wore Historically Black College and University sweatshirts during the fall and winter because wearing dashikis was impractical in cold temperatures. "What's been goin' on?"

While I felt empowered by my new status at school, the things that made me popular were not things I wanted to share with Blackmun. I avoided the question and explained in garbled tones that I hadn't been around because I felt uncomfortable about coming by after the incident with the photograph.

"Oh, I didn't mind the photo, but I did mind the disrespect," Blackmun said. "But long, long—long ago, much longer than you can imagine, I was a teenager, also, believe it or not, sooooooooo..."—he punctuated his sentence with a smile and a knowing wink—"you and your friends are always welcome here." Then he added with a laugh, "Of course, I'm still not going to take no mess from y'all."

Moments of awkward silence followed as I nervously shifted my eyes around the store. I was about to speak. I wanted to talk about Grandma's new job and how I resented her telling me to stay home and look after the twins—as if I were a child myself. But I said nothing. Blackmun seemed to sense my anger at the injustice of my situation.

"What's bothering you, Son?" Blackmun gently asked. I wanted to talk but still said nothing. I wanted to tell Blackmun about the overwhelming power I now felt at school, especially when I was next to J.J. My classmates had always tolerated, even respected me as a nerd, especially since I had some athletic ability. But now they admired me. I was one of the cool kids. I wanted to tell Blackmun how mad I was at Grandma, who expected me to accept so many responsibilities without complaint. Finally, I blurted out that I felt Grandma treated me like a kid.

Blackmun let my resentful words subside, then, leaning over the counter with exaggerated confidentiality, said, "I wasn't always a black man, you know." His eyes seemed to dance with delight as he peered at me, a smile playing on his lips.

I studied Blackmun's face, his 4C hair, dark brown skin, and full lips. I wondered if my new friends weren't right after all—maybe Blackmun was demented, or senile, or crazy, or just a fool.

For his part, Blackmun seemed to be enjoying my confusion. He rolled up the sleeves of the olive drab sweatshirt he wore up to his elbows. He passed each hand up and down over the opposite arm's expanse of exposed skin, then opened his hands wide, directly in front of my face, like a magician about to perform a miraculous trick.

"This," Blackmun said, glancing at his exposed skin, "is not what makes me a black man." He paused dramatically. "*This* is," he said, tapping the fingers of his right hand to his heart. "And *this*," he said, tapping those fingers to his temple. "My skin color just gives me a head start," he said playfully.

Blackmun then pulled his sleeves down and looked at me, and suddenly he was no longer playful.

"There comes a time in every black person's life when he or she arrives at a crossroads," Blackmun said, staring at me to gauge the effect of his words. "There comes a time in black people's lives when they have to decide what *they* mean when they say they are black, when they say that they are of African heritage. Is it merely a matter of skin color and hair texture? What will they make that skin color and hair texture—that heritage—*mean*? Is it something to live up to or something to live down? When they arrive at that crossroads, most people aren't even aware of it, but that doesn't make it any less real. You, Miles, are now at that crossroads."

I clenched my jaw in anger. It sounded to me like Blackmun was challenging my racial pride. Dad had always made a point of teaching the twins and me about black history—and not just during Black History Month. Blackmun, who had had countless conversations with my father, should know that, I reasoned. I could feel myself getting angrier by the second. No, I hadn't grown up "hard" in the "'hood," but I was no stranger to anger and injustice. As I continued to reflect on what Blackmun might be driving at, I felt anger rise from deep within me, and my hands balled into hard, tight fists. After all, I could tick off a list of black "firsts" without even trying—first black astronaut in space, Guy Bluford, Jr.; first black member of the U.S. Supreme Court, Thurgood Marshall; first black woman elected to the United States Congress, Shirley Chisholm.

I had several T-shirts with images of the Motherland on them and wore them often and proudly. I could count to ten in Swahili, and last semester at the school talent show, I even recited by heart all of Gil Scott-Heron's acerbic "Whitey on the Moon" and accompanied myself on bongos!

"Nobody tells me what it means to be black," I fumed, with an intensity that surprised even me.

"What you mean is that nobody but you *should* tell you what it means to be black," Blackmun corrected patiently. "You already have millions of people telling you. They're coming at you from all sides all the time and have been doing so since before you drew your first breath and will continue long after you've drawn your last. They come at you from radio and television programs, from magazine and newspaper articles, and from movies. No matter how many black anchors you see on news shows, no matter how many black men and women appear on the covers of magazines on newsstands, the behavior of clerks towards you in stores and from casual comments and attitudes from oblivious teachers, administrators, classmates, and staff at school are telling you what it means to be black.

"The cop with a crew cut who stops you on a bone-chilling winter's day because a black person walking with his bare hands in his pockets looks 'sus-pi-ci-ous'; the East Indian restaurant owner who walks over to your table and 'shushes' you and your family for 'laughing too loudly'; the Asian woman who reflexively clutches her blond boyfriend's arm for dear life when you sit next to them at a movie theater, all of them are telling you what it means to be black. As a race—as an ethnic group—we're basically on our own. Our hair, our lips, our gums, the melanin in the lines of our palms, our skin color are often the butt of 'didn't *mean* to be offensive' jokes. Even now, only weeks before the dawn of the twenty-first century, the efforts by others to define our blackness—and to diminish us with that definition—remain relentless.

"Look, Miles, I'm not telling you what it means to be black," Blackmun continued. "I'm not telling you that you are two shades too light or that you are two shades too dark." He walked around from behind the counter and ushered me the few steps to the front door of his shop. Then, as he put his comforting hand on my shoulder, he said, "I'm not telling you what to be or to do anything in particular. I'm simply trying to jog your memory by making a general observation. You are at a crossroads. It's a crossroads we all come to.

"Think about what I said, about coming to this crossroads. We all need support when we reach it. In the kente cloth, I have given you a device—a tool. But remember: the menu is not the meal, the reflection is not the object reflected, and the symbol is not the thing symbolized. And continue to remember,"

Blackmun said, "that my door is always open to you. If you need my help, just call. Anytime. Because we're in this together."

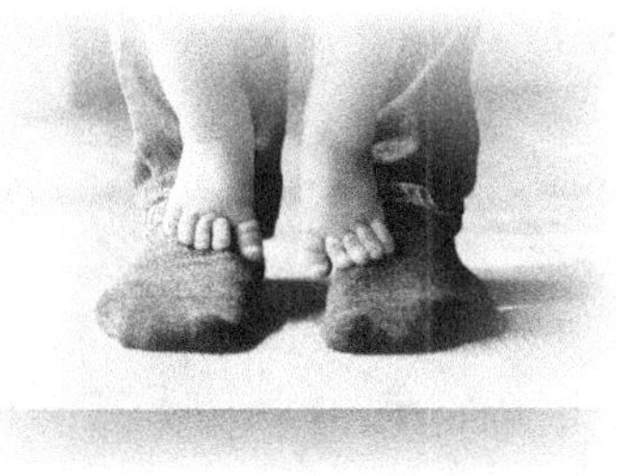

UP IN SMOKE

The intoxicating and noxious mixture of fumes from spray paint, felt-tipped markers, and glue filled the basement of our house. Assembled there were me, J.J., and the twins, whose school art project was the source of the fumes. Grandma wouldn't return until much later. I climbed the few steps to the closed, metal double doors that led to the back-yard and pushed them open. A rush of cold November night air swept in, clearing everyone's head.

I propped open the doors a crack with a nearby metal rod, then returned down the stairs. The extra refrigerator stood directly across from me. I opened its door, revealing a colorful trove of canned and bottled sodas, juices, and carbonated water. I took out a couple of cans of cola and walked over to J.J., who was sitting on one of two folding chairs in front of the washer and dryer on one side of the room. I handed him a can and plopped down beside him on the second folding chair. We popped the tabs of our cans, which hissed open, and looked in the general direction of my siblings at the opposite side of the room.

The twins had laid out their school project on a card table they were sharing. Their task was to research the traditional meaning of the colors and patterns used in kente cloth designs. Next, they were to create a design out of paint, construction paper, and wrapping paper that would express something they wanted to say about themselves, their family, or their culture.

Douglass knew that he was looking for something that spoke about power, like the comic book superheroes such as Falcon and Black Panther he enjoyed reading about. Ida, with Halloween still on her mind, was thinking of ghosts. And so, the twins' designs would look very different as they progressed. But both patterns were going to be laced with gold, which Ida and Douglass had learned represented prosperity, royalty, and the influence of God in human life. They also personalized the meaning as a reminder of our late parents. But right now, any higher meaning—personal, traditional, or cultural—was obscured by their squabbling with each other over who would get to use the measly foot-square sheet of gold wrapping paper. I snapped at them to shut up, then stomped over to the table and snatched away the source of the conflict.

I am embarrassed to say I had been curt with the twins throughout the afternoon, especially when they asked me for help with their project. When Ida asked me what a particular word in the book she was using to research her design meant, I'm ashamed to say I gruffly replied, "Look it up yourself." When Douglass told me he and Ida had borrowed the kente cloth Blackmun had given me to copy one of its patterns, I barely listened. Instead, I cut him off and brusquely ordered him to "Be quiet and finish your project!" By the time J.J. dropped by in the early evening, I was in a foul mood and had let him know why.

When I walked back from the refrigerator to J.J., he whispered, "My man, don't let nobody, even your grandma, clown you, tell you what to do, who to be, where you're at. As long as you let everybody push you around, they're going to push you around some more." He punctuated this revelation by taking a glug of his soda.

I thought about what he said for a second; it seemed to make sense.

"Stand up for yourself, dawg," J.J. continued. "Stop acting like a kid, and they'll stop treating you like one." J.J. took another swig, then leaned closer to me and said in a hushed tone, "I wouldn't be your boy if I didn't tell you this, but people are laughing at you behind your back."

J.J. didn't say which people. His beeper went off, with its piercing rhythmic trill. He pulled it from his waistband, took a quick look at it, then returned it to the waistband.

"Listen, LaShawn's parents are out of town, and in about an hour, some of us are getting together at his crib. You gotta be there, Son. Talk to some honeys, get your swerve on. Just put the twins to bed and swing by. They won't miss you because they'll be asleep, and you'll be back before your grandmother comes home. It'll be butter." He paused dramatically, then added. "On the real, man, you've got to hang! People are starting to forget that you're alive!"

A party sounded like a great idea to me. After the past few weeks that I had been stuck babysitting evenings, I wanted excitement. And I wouldn't mind basking in the newfound admiration from my classmates beyond the walls of our school.

J.J.'s beeper went off again. He glanced down at it without pulling it out of his waistband this time. He stood up and put his soda on the seat.

"Look, I gotta jet," he said, grabbing his jacket, draped on the back of his chair. As he slipped it on, I stood up and put my soda on the seat of my chair. I led J.J. to the heavy basement doors, pushed them open, and we emerged outside. "Holla at me," he said as we dapped. He turned to his lime-green Haro Master BMX bike, which he had laid on its side next to the basement doors.

"Yeah, later," I replied. J.J. reached down, righted his bike, and jumped onto it. He pedaled a couple of strokes, popped his front tire into a quick wheelie before making a crunching, crackling sound that diminished as he rolled over our gravel driveway off our property. I went back down the steps into the basement, closed the doors so they remained open a crack, then returned to my seat by the washer and dryer. I swooped my half-empty soda can up from the seat of the folding chair, drained it with a few aggressive chugs, then slammed my butt down on the chair and glared at my siblings, who were glumly absorbed in their projects. The muffled sound of crinkling aluminum rose from my lap as my hands tightened around the now empty soda can.

I stared a hole in the clock on the wall behind my brother and sister. The clock's thin brass hands were attached to a foot-and-a-half-long piece of mahogany carved in the shape of Africa. Watching those hands move was like watching icicles melt on the coldest February day—in other words, the hands seemed not to move forward at all. At times, they seemed to click backward.

Finally, after an interminable half-hour, the hands read eight o'clock. I sprang from my chair and sped across the basement to lock the outside basement door when they did. I then turned to Ida and Douglass, who were still working on their project, and crisply ordered them to get ready for bed.

"Why do we have to go to bed now?" asked Douglass incredulously. "It's Friday. We never go to bed this early on Fridays and Saturdays."

"Just do what I say," I growled, and they both reluctantly rose to their feet.

"But it's too early for us to go to *sleep*," Ida said, using all her effort to assert herself. "Why do we have to go to bed now!? We'll just end up staying awake playing or talking."

She shrank away, a little fearful, it seemed to me, when I suddenly moved toward her and her twin brother. I swung around behind them and put a firm hand on each of their backs.

"No, you won't," I said impatiently while guiding them, none too gently, away from their crafts table, through the basement, up its steps, and through the house to their bedroom on the second floor. "You guys have been cranky all day," I continued. "You need your rest. I'm sure you'll both go to sleep right away. So please," I added, irritated, "go and get ready for bed and stop giving me a hard time." Hearing no hint of compromise in my voice, the twins trudged the rest of the way to their bedroom without me nudging them forward with my hands.

After the twins were brushed, washed, in their pajamas, and in bed, I decided to close their bedroom door, which was usually left open. I wanted to make sure they wouldn't hear the back door shut when I left the house or hear my footsteps and the wheels of my bike as I walked it over our gravel driveway. But when I gently pulled the door closed, Douglass and Ida panicked.

"Don't shut our door!" Douglass pleaded.

I swung the door open and clomped back into the room. "I have to," I barked. "I'm going to listen to my music on the stereo, and I don't want to keep you up."

"Use your Walkman; put on your earphones," Ida implored, pointing to my neck, where the earphones rested as usual.

"I don't want to," I said, with no attempt to hide my annoyance.

"But I'm scared," Ida persisted.

"Look," I said, impatiently, "there's nothing to be scared of, but if you need some comfort, get one of your dolls and snuggle with it. Really. It will be all right. I'm going to shut the door. I want to listen to music on the stereo. You'll be all right. Now—Go! To! Sleep! *Pleeeease!*" I walked out of the room, pulling the door behind me just short of slamming it shut. I was about to run down the stairs but abruptly stopped for a long moment. I thought I had forgotten something, but I couldn't figure out what. I continued down the stairs, assuming that it would eventually come to me if it were something important. I slipped out the back door, hopped on my bicycle, and pedaled the ten minutes to the party.

I skidded to a stop in LaShawn's driveway near about a half dozen other bikes. I hopped off and lifted my right foot to push down my kickstand when my heart skipped a beat. I now remembered—I hadn't said our family's special prayers for my brother and sister. That had never happened before. Dad had recited that prayer, which ended, "Thank you for giving my son, Miles, a strong mind and a strong, healthy body," to me every night without fail until I was at least ten years old, even over the phone when Dad was away on business. Every night I had babysat my siblings, I had remembered to say the same prayer to them, ending it, "Thank you for giving my brother, Douglass, and sister, Ida, strong minds and strong, healthy bodies." And I knew Grandma *never* forgot the twins' special prayers when she was in charge. My little sister and brother must have been so panicked when I shut the door that they failed to remind me. I hopped off my bike and walked as if I were in a trance towards LaShawn's house, stopping just short of its closed front door.

I raised my index finger. It hovered an indecisive inch or two from the doorbell button. I flirted with the idea of going back home. But the twins were probably asleep by now. No matter. It would be all right. My finger slowly moved towards the button. It paused again. What if they were still awake and calling out for me? What if they got out of bed and were wandering alone around the house looking for me? What if, fearing something terrible had happened to me, they picked up the phone and called the neighbors? What if they called Grandma at work? Perhaps I should rethink this situation. Maybe I should bag this adventure and head back home. Then my index finger traveled with the irreversible direction and speed of a bullet blasting from the barrel of a pistol. Its target—the beckoning dim light of the doorbell button; upon contact, a disconcertingly loud "ding-dong," like the chimes of Big Ben, resonated throughout the front porch. A few moments later, the front door swung open, and a smiling LaShawn greeted me. He wore overalls he had dyed green and on which he had silk-screened scores of images of hundred-dollar bills, with multitudinous faces of Ben Franklin gazing out with an enigmatic expression. Beneath the overalls, LaShawn wore a Henley shirt he had tie-dyed lavender and yellow.

"Yo, dawg!" said LaShawn, whose thin box braids dangled to his shoulders. Ever the rebel, LaShawn had decided to decorate his locks with safety pins rather than the beads one would have expected. I should say here that LaShawn was white—specifically, a mixture of Irish and Italian American. But he seemed to have an affinity for black people, at least at that time. He was up on the most current black music, style, and lingo. In middle school, he had given himself what he called a "soul" name that he said fit his personality better than Brad, the name his parents had given him. However, by his junior year of high school, he had reverted to his given name and capitalized on his idealized frat boy looks—square jaw, perfect teeth, blue-gray eyes, sandy-brown hair—with a body destined for the lacrosse field. But as a freshman in high school, he had continued to remedy his pasty complexion by exposing as much skin as possible to the sun playing pickup basketball games outdoors in the warmer months. Even now, in November, he retained enough of his tan (with a little bronzer) to pass as a light-skinned "brotha." At our school, he was one of several nonblack "Afro-wannabes," but my black friends froze them out of conversations when they sat at our lunch table; for some reason they welcomed LaShawn as "one of us." If this evening's invitation list echoed those of his previous parties, he would be the only white person there. I never figured out what to make of that...

LaShawn gave me a hearty dap and shoulder-bang hug, then gushed, "Come on in!" I hesitated again. I felt another pang of guilt about the twins, but it was fainter this time. Barely noticeable. My feet rose a millimeter or two off the ground, and I floated over the front door threshold towards LaShawn. We drifted through the house's short portal into the living room, through a door into LaShawn's family's den, where I landed, ready to plunge into the party.

Well, it wasn't really a party. It was a bunch of kids standing around looking uncomfortable in the yellowish-brown half-light cast by a pair of lamps. The lamps sat on coffee tables at either end of a wall to the right of where we entered. Ten or so girls stood on one side of the room and about the same number of boys stood on the other side. Everybody seemed to cast their gaze at the floor, the walls, the ceiling—just about anything so long as it didn't have a pulse. No doubt, they were all trying to figure out how to make their first move. A couple of the guys noticed me when I entered and nodded but did no more than that. One of the girls saw me and giggled.

A stereo system, located between the two lamps, was tuned to a radio station playing a commercial for a tire company. When I didn't see J.J., I turned to tell LaShawn I had to roll when J.J. came striding through the swinging door that led from the kitchen to the den. He shouted, "Yo, let's get it started." His mere arrival seemed to electrify the atmosphere. He headed straight to the stereo, turned off the radio, and popped in a cassette of what I assumed was a mixtape he had created. Whoever made it or wherever it came from, the mixtape kicked off with the bangin' "Humpty Dance" by Digital Underground with its P-Funk bass that immediately got everybody's body cranking. In a matter of minutes after he had shown up, J.J. had lit up the party.

After three hours, I figured I'd better head back home. I didn't want to push my luck about when Grandma would return. I looked around the den to tell J.J. I was leaving. When I didn't see him there, I went through the swinging door into the kitchen, which was illuminated only by the range light over the stove. I spotted J.J. and a girl. They both leaned with their backs against the counter across from the oven. She was svelte and nearly as tall as J.J. She wore a simple headwrap of indeterminate color in the low light. One of his arms gently fell over her shoulders. Their faces were inches from one another. She punctuated her shy smiles with sips of soda from a straw stuck into a can, hoping to camouflage her evident excitement, I assumed. He didn't return her smile but maintained steady eye contact.

"Yo, J.J.," I said softly; I didn't want to break the romantic spell it looked like he was weaving. "I've gotta bounce," I said. "Thanks for inviting me."

He looked at me briefly, offered a perfunctory nod, and returned his attention to the girl. "No problem, catch ya later," he said mechanically.

As I headed out of the kitchen, I heard J.J. call out: "Yo, Miles." I turned around. "I'm glad you made it," he said with a sincere smile.

When I got home, I looked at the microwave's clock in the kitchen. Just before midnight, a cool half hour before Grandma usually returned home. I buttered a slice of bread, poured myself a glass of milk, and carried them as I made my way toward the stairs to my bedroom. Things had gone so smoothly, I thought perhaps I would make a habit of going out while my brother and sister were asleep. As I climbed the stairs, I smelled something. Breadcrumbs had gotten stuck in the toaster oven again, I figured, until I realized I hadn't toasted my bread. I looked up to my left. The twins' door was ajar. Hadn't I shut it when I left? I noticed a ghostly tongue of smoke rising from under the door to their room. I dropped my food and bounded up the remaining steps to the landing.

I flung open the door to my siblings' bedroom. Smoke billowed towards me. My brother and sister lay motionless in their separate beds. A smattering of embers smoldered at the foot of Douglass's goosedown duvet. When I tore the cover off Douglass, a mesmerizing chaos of glowing cinders swirled into the air around me like hundreds of fireflies. Douglass didn't move. I looked at his bed and saw smoke rising from an electric blanket near the foot of the bed. It had shorted. I ripped it off the bed and saw a circle of orange embers where the hot metal wires had begun to burn into the mattress.

One at a time, I lifted my siblings from their respective beds. I felt as if I were lifting fifty-pound sacks of potatoes. Neither stirred. My heart pounded as I carried them into the hall and set them on the floor against the wall near the stair landing. They gradually came around. Groggy from smoke and sleep, a series of hacking coughs poured out of them as they gasped for air. They were alive! I dashed back into the room, checked quickly to ensure nothing was on fire, unplugged the blanket, then grabbed their coats from their closet. When I returned to the landing, the twins were sobbing. Douglass repeatedly said, "I'm sorry, Miles." I had told my brother on a previous occasion not to plug in the old electric blanket. Tonight, I knelt beside him and held his hand to reassure him that I wasn't angry. I helped my siblings stand up, gathered their coats under one of my arms, and guided them down the stairs away from the smoke, which had swelled out of the room like fog into the entire second floor. I told them to put their coats on over their pajamas and wait for me on the front porch. I went to the kitchen and called the fire department. I also tried to reach Grandma at her job. When the operator said she had left for the night, I tried Grandma's cell phone. No answer, so I left a message, trying to sound calm but asking her to call me right away.

When I rushed to the front door, I saw Ida was still inside, struggling to put on her coat. She was having trouble threading one of her hands through her sleeve; that hand clutched the kente cloth Blackmun had given me at Dad's funeral. It was singed. I gently pried the fabric from my sister's hand and tossed it back into the house, where it landed in a corner of the entrance hallway. I then helped my sister put on her coat and ushered her into the cold, where we all waited for the firefighters to arrive.

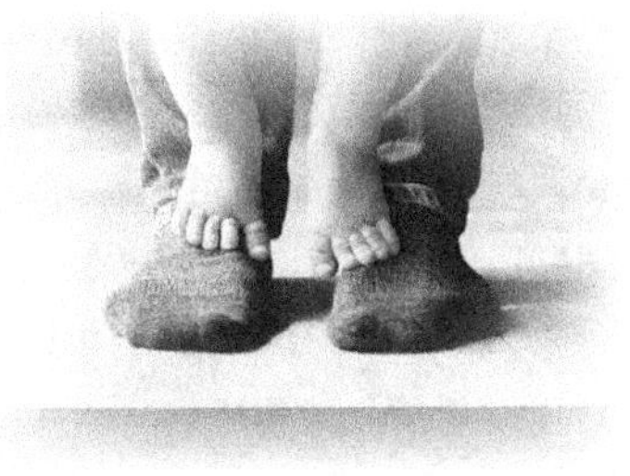

THE ACCIDENTAL HERO

"**W**hatcha readin', brothas?" asked Blackmun the next day. "I heard you were a hero last night." Blackmun raised his hand to give me five. It was Saturday midafternoon, and Blackmun had been sweeping the sidewalk in front of his store when he saw J.J. and me walk by. We were so involved in our conversation that Blackmun had taken us by surprise. We both fidgeted with discomfort—me because I knew not only was I not a hero, I almost caused my brother's and sister's deaths; J.J. because he had told me many times since his last encounter with Blackmun that he hated having to listen to "that crazy jerk."

I unenthusiastically extended my hand, palm up, to receive Blackmun's five and responded that I was not a hero. "Everyone in the family was just lucky last night."

"Well, your grandmother dropped by to pick up a paper earlier, and she called you a hero," Blackmun said, giving me a congratulatory smile. I remembered the conversation with Grandma the night before, how she had come home to find me with the twins safely outside, the ambulance and fire truck arriving roughly when she did. I remembered how relieved Grandma was that everybody was safe. (It turned out that Douglass had been cold. After calling out for me many times, he went to the linen closet, retrieved the old electric blanket, and plugged it in even though he knew he wasn't supposed to. I lied to Grandma and told her I was in the basement, not out of the house, and that was why I hadn't heard Douglass calling for an extra blanket. I didn't share those details with Blackmun.)

But as Blackmun continued to look at me, his smile dimmed. He cocked his head a bit to his right and squinted as if trying to bring a distant object into focus. He held that pose for a quiet moment. As he did, I had the strange sensation of something moving around inside me, near my belly button—as if billiard balls were scattering and clacking around after a break shot. It wasn't a pleasant feeling, but it wasn't unpleasant, either. Mostly, it was unsettling.

"Anyway," Blackmun said at last, "it's a good thing you were there and woke them up in time."

Then he invited us into his store for a free juice or soda.

"Come on, it'll be on me. Think of it as a reward," Blackmun said.

J.J. seemed to relax after seeing Blackmun was not going to pick up where their previous encounter left off. He explained that we had to catch a bus to the city to check out sound equipment for the music group we planned to form. The twins had spent the night in the hospital for observation. Grandma decided to take the day off to make sure they rested at home, which meant she didn't need to take a nap before going to work that evening, and I was free to join J.J. for the whole day.

"Well, come on inside, grab something to drink, and take it with you," Blackmun insisted. "About when will the bus arrive?"

"In about twenty-five minutes," I said.

"Well then, you have plenty of time. It's only a five-minute walk to the bus stop. Come on in," said Blackmun, leading the way.

Inside the shop, Blackmun handed us the apple juice and grape soda we had requested. "Tell me about this group. Do you have a name?"

"Not yet, but we're working on it. Miles wants to come up with the beats," J.J. said.

"Beatmaster J, kickin' it old school," I said, laughing because I knew how corny I sounded.

"And I like to rap," J.J. added. "But we thought we might get another rapper, possibly a girl."

"I've already got a pretty good twelve-inch collection and one turntable," I volunteered. "I just need to get a laptop and some software for more beats and effects. There are a couple of stores in the city that are supposed to have pretty good deals."

"Before you get yourself on the cover of Vibe magazine, you'll need to find out how much the equipment costs," Blackmun said. "And once you figure that out, where are you going to get the money?"

The question took me by surprise. In the initial rush of wanting to start a group, I had overlooked that fundamental question. "W-w-well," I stuttered, "I-I have some savings." But even as I said it, I knew that the meager amount I had wouldn't begin to cover the cost of the equipment I needed. I began to wonder if maybe I turned up my nose at that lemonade stand money too soon.

"Listen," Blackmun said, reading the confusion on my face. "If you need work, let's talk. I don't need help around the store right now, but if you're good with a lawnmower, maybe we can work out something. You know," Blackmun mused out loud, picking up steam, "I don't suppose there's any harm in letting a thirteen-year-old get a little entrepreneurial experience. I own a two-family house on Appleton Place. Since it's near Thanksgiving, you can rake the remaining leaves, clean gutters, and help me with the odd maintenance on the property. Come spring, there'll be grass in need of mowing, weeds to pull, hedges to trim. I can pay you...eight dollars an hour for a few hours over the weekends. That's more than minimum wage. In a couple of months, you can save enough to help you launch your music career."

Upon hearing that, J.J. doubled over with laughter. "Man, that's chump change."

Blackmun pursed his lips in disapproval and was about to say something when a woman in her early twenties entered the store. A Lauryn Hill lookalike, she had twisted her hair into dark tendrils that cascaded down either side of her face. She wore a black leotard top, layered with an untucked black-and-red checkered flannel shirt, and a shearling bomber jacket. Slouchy dungarees and a pair of Timbs 6-inch work boots completed the look. Upon seeing Blackmun, she lit up with delight.

"Qué estás leyendo?" she asked before kissing him on the cheek. He gave her an avuncular hug and said, "I'm peepin' fierce knowledge, baby. *Fierce!*"

Releasing her from his gentle embrace, he said, "Yo, baby girl, let me introduce you to these young men. Miles, J.J.—Freedom. Freedom—Miles and J.J."

She looked at me and J.J., and her smile subtly but perceptibly faded. She extended her hand to shake ours but leaned back ever so slightly as if distancing herself from an unpleasant odor.

"Freedom Sommers," she said with a chilliness that contrasted with the warmth she showed Blackmun. "Good to meet you," she added unconvincingly.

Either ignoring or unaware of Freedom's reaction to me and J.J., Blackmun interjected, "Freedom, these young men just told me they want to start a music group. Guys, Freedom is in law school and studying to specialize in entertainment law when she graduates. You all should get together—have coffee, hang out in a park...get to know each other."

Freedom gave J.J. and me a wan smile and abruptly turned her attention back to Blackmun. She said she had a lot of errands to run that day, led Blackmun to a far corner of the shop, leaned in close to him, and began speaking rapidly in Spanish.

J.J. stealthily motioned for me to join him near the magazines, where he was standing, and pulled out a copy of *Ebony* with Queen Latifah on the cover. He opened it to some random article, which we gazed at blindly.

"What's she saying?" he whispered urgently.

I understood some Spanish because my mother and her side of the family were Afro-Latinos from Colombia. My middle name is my mother's maiden name—de la Esperanza. After Mom died, my father continued our annual two-week visits to Bogotá during the Christmas or Easter holidays, or my maternal grandparents, who didn't speak English, would visit the U.S. There were also regular phone calls. But my last visit had been three years earlier, shortly before my maternal grandmother died. My maternal grandfather was too frail to travel and beset by severe dementia, making it difficult for him to speak or understand any language. So my Spanish was rusty.

Freedom spoke quickly and in a murmur. She drew an envelope from her jacket. From what I could gather, Freedom's great-aunt was one of Blackmun's tenants. I found out later that as a child of the Great Depression, she didn't trust banks and paid her rent—and just about everything else—in cash. Today she had to attend a can't-miss church meeting, Freedom said, but because the rent was due, she had asked her great-niece to bring it. Freedom added with a laugh that it was also an excellent opportunity for a quick visit. She broke into English, saying she had aced all her law courses. "Dónde está mi dinero, eh, Papi!?" she asked, rubbing her thumb and forefinger together in a money-grubbing gesture.

"It's on its way," Blackmun said, and they both broke out laughing.

After Freedom left, I said to Blackmun, "I never knew before today that you're a landlord."

Blackmun smiled broadly. Putting the envelope in a drawer under the counter, he said proudly, "It was a good investment." He glanced at J.J. but directed his comment at me. "You should never be afraid to start small. It helped me get to where I am today."

"Blackmun, you own a two-bit candy store and a small, old, two-family house—*biiiig* freakin' deal," said J.J., who had either lost his mind or forgotten that Blackmun could unleash a world of hurt.

But Blackmun just shook his head. "The trouble is, J.J., it's your *thinking* that's small."

J.J. joked, "Hey, I'm all about the Benjamins. Money's cool, yo. Just don't act like no Bill Gates."

Blackmun's cell phone rang. He took his Motorola StarTAC out of its case, which he had clamped to his belt, and flipped it open like a crew member from the T.V. show *Star Trek*. After glancing at the number, he said, "Whatcha readin', lady?" and after a couple of seconds, he put the caller on hold. "If anyone comes in, tell them I'll be right back," Blackmun said, then continued the phone conversation as he disappeared down the steps behind the counter into the basement.

J.J. leaned over to me and pointed with his chin in the direction of the envelope.

"I've got the answer to your money worries, Miles," he said in a hoarse whisper. I couldn't believe J.J. was talking about stealing from Blackmun. After my narrow escape from the night before, I felt I had courted enough danger for the time being. Besides, Blackmun was my friend. And beyond that, I knew it was just plain wrong. I glanced over to the stairs where Blackmun had disappeared, then back at J.J., who broke into a smile. He seemed to be able to read the signs of anxiety on my face. I looked towards the stairs again.

"I wouldn't steer you wrong," J.J. said reassuringly. "There are no lives at stake here. It's just some easy cash, probably more than you'd get in a month of pulling weeds and shoveling snow! The money in that drawer there—it will help you get to where you want to go."

My fear of catastrophe lessened, but a solid wall of conscience kept me from seriously entertaining the idea. J.J. seemed to intuit his partial victory. "Listen," J.J. whispered intently, accelerating his momentum, "Blackmun just lives off black people the way white people do. What's the big deal? That he gives you a buck for your 'good' grades? Those lame black pride displays he puts in his windows?"

I had never considered this before, but my friend seemed to have thought it all out. J.J. took another swig of his soda and made a disdainful face. "He's just a crazy old man—he'll probably never even miss it."

Clearly, I remember thinking, this was a test. J.J. could easily steal the money himself, but he was prodding me to take it.

"Blackmun trusts you, Miles," J.J. pointed out. "He'll never even come looking in your direction. Or maybe," he continued, "you just don't have the guts." He chugged his remaining soda and crushed the can. "Maybe I had you all wrong. Maybe you are still a kid." He said no more, just rotated the crushed soda can in his hand and stared at me.

"OK," I said.

J.J. smiled and nodded. "You down, then," he stated.

"I'm down," I confirmed.

Blackmun returned from the basement as he was finishing his call. He flipped his phone shut and returned it to its case on his hip, then suddenly snapped his fingers in irritation and muttered to himself, "I forgot to give her a receipt."

He pulled out the envelope with the rent money from the drawer under the counter and started to put it in his back pocket. I felt a wave of relief. How could I make off with the money if he had it on him and took it to who knows where? But just then, his phone rang again, and he absentmindedly returned the money to the drawer and took the call. "Whatcha readin', baby!" he said, and while the person on the end of the line responded, Blackmun mouthed, "Catch you later," and waved goodbye to me and J.J. as we headed off towards the bus stop.

But after walking a ways from the store, J.J. stopped and looked at me. "We have to come up with a plan," he said.

We decided we would pretend to go to the bus. J.J. would go home and stay there. I would circle back to the store and establish a spot to scope out the store without arousing suspicion. When Blackmun went down to the basement, as he often did, I could sneak in and take the money from the drawer. The only thing that could go wrong would be if he caught me with my hand in the till, so to speak, but I could reduce the chances of that by listening for his footsteps coming up the basement stairs and by being quick. After all, I knew where the money should be located. If Blackmun caught me in the store, no problem, I'd just say there was a change of plans, and I decided to return to buy some chips. And as J.J. said, once he noticed the money was gone, he'd never suspect me. Besides, Blackmun had a reputation in town for occasionally being absentminded or at least seeming to be that way. Who knows, he might not even notice the money was missing or think it was all a figment of one of his "spells." That was our thinking, anyway.

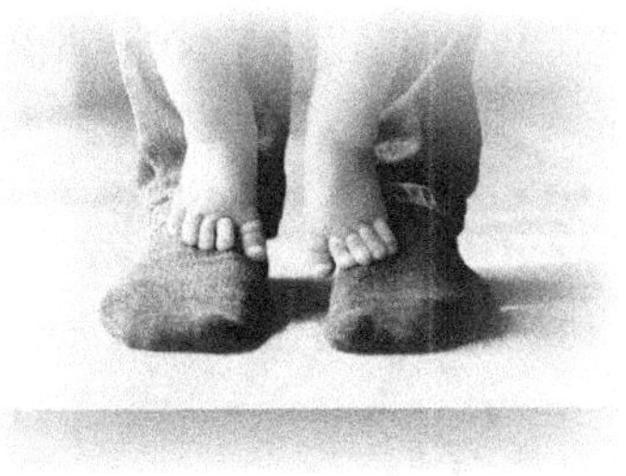

EYELESS

Later that day, Grandma, the twins, and I were in our kitchen. Eerily, Dad's outgoing message was still on the answering machine, and we decided to replace it with a new message. Grandma and I were trying to help the twins craft it. But every time I pointed my finger, meaning "Start now," Ida became tongue-tied, no matter how well she had rehearsed. And Douglass, who switched words in his part of the greeting—changing "residence" to "home" to "domicile"—did not help her.

The doorbell rang, and I volunteered to get it. When I opened the front door, J.J. was standing there.

"Well? Did you get the money?" J.J. asked.

I shushed him, but he persisted.

"Yeah, yeah," I finally said. "Now get out of here. It's a bad time," and I started to shut the door.

J.J. put his foot out, where it met the closing door with a soft thump. "So, where is it?" he asked.

"Who is it, Miles?" Grandma called out from the kitchen.

I ignored her and spoke to J.J. from the narrow opening between the door and the doorframe. "Up-stairs," I hissed. "I hid it."

J.J. looked at his foot caught between the door and the doorframe and then at me. "That's cold-blooded, Bro," he quietly deadpanned before smiling sarcastically and withdrawing his foot.

The next day was Sunday, and as usual, I went to church with Grandma, Douglass, and Ida. After the service, huddled figures scurried down the church steps, making their way along the sidewalk and into their cars to escape the late November chill. As my family and I left the warmth and the sweet smell of frankincense of the church, I noticed there was a still figure leaning against a utility pole directly in front of us. When I recognized the figure as J.J., I averted my eyes and quickened my pace down the steps.

"Isn't that your friend J.J.?" Grandma asked as I tugged her so we would meet the sidewalk several feet away from the motionless figure.

"Yeah," I replied crossly, scrunching up my shoulders as if protecting myself from the cold. I turned away from J.J. as much as possible without being too obvious. But I could sense J.J. following me with his eyes. I glanced back at him, and he gave me a reptilian smile.

That Monday at noon, I sat at the corner of a

lunch table by myself, but I was soon joined by J.J., who gave me a robust slap on the back before sliding down next to me on the bench. "Which laptop are you going to buy?" he asked me. At this point, three of our friends joined us: one was light-skinned and heavyset with reddish hair; one was gaunt, tall, and dark; and the third was a boy of medium color and build who had a shaved head.

"I'm not so sure that I'm going to buy one," I said.

J.J. looked surprised. "Why not? That's why you took the money, isn't it?" His eyes narrowed. "You did take the money, didn't you?"

"Yes, I did," I said curtly. "I just don't know what I want to buy with it."

"What money are you talking about?" asked the heavyset boy with the café au lait complexion and reddish hair. J.J. filled everybody in.

"Yo, how much did you get?" the teen with the shaved head asked.

"Five hundred dollars," J.J. volunteered for me. Of course, neither he nor I knew how much money was there. I figured J.J. had chosen a random number as a test, to see how I'd react. I decided to roll with it.

"Man, that's a good take," the tall, dark boy said with admiration.

"Yeah, but homey here got scared and almost punked out," J.J. said.

I immediately refuted J.J.; I felt my manhood was being attacked. "I wasn't scared, and I didn't almost punk out," I asserted vehemently, and then found myself bragging about how clever the theft had been, how I'd waited patiently for the right moment for Blackmun to disappear into his basement and for the store to be free of customers. How I'd darted into the store, alert to passersby on the street who might see me entering or leaving. How I'd rehearsed in my head what I would say if he caught me in the store, and even what I'd say if he caught me red-handed. How I debated whether to take only the rent money or clear out the cash register to make sure the crime seemed random. (I told my friends I decided to take only the rent money. He'd surely notice an empty till, but knowing he was prone to "spells," I thought he might forget that he had even received the rent.)

On Wednesday, two days later, shortly after the beginning of my last-period class, my teacher told me to see the principal. When I arrived at his office, the secretary nodded towards an inner door with a rectangle of frosted glass with gold decal letters reading James P. Washington, with his title under it. I knocked on the door, opened it, and entered. Mr. Washington, half sitting on the front edge of his large, standard-issue wooden principal's desk, pointed to one of two tan plastic chairs in front of it. "Have a seat," he said.

Mr. Washington was imposing, especially when he stood—not because of his height, however, which was average, but because of the physicality he radiated. Perhaps this force came from him being a former athlete, a wide receiver for Grambling State. But his college career was cut short, and dreams of playing for the NFL were crushed when a car hit him in a crosswalk as he made his way across the street. He still limped slightly, and it was more pronounced when it rained.

He could be pretentious, with the pompous bearing of a bureaucrat. Teachers and students alike ridiculed him behind his back for his ridiculously precise "dic-tion" and his showy and seemingly unnecessary use of big words, for instance, saying "cacophonous" when "noisy" would do. But everyone acknowledged that he was an effective and tireless champion on behalf of all his students. He used his parliamentary demeanor and keen grant-writing skills to get money for our school's countless extra programs and equipment.

Mr. Washington looked at me as if sizing me up before deciding what to say first. Finally, he simply said, "There's been a robbery. Somebody stole hundreds of dollars over the weekend from the convenience store, the one on Walnut and Chestnut." I felt my heart pound. "Do you know anything about this?"

I shook my head. Principal Washington explained that on Monday, there were rumors that someone burglarized Blackmun. After confirming it with Blackmun, the town's school superintendent asked the principals of the high school and the two junior high schools to discreetly ask around to see if any students had information about the crime. He went on to say that three freshmen boys at our school—friends of mine—had been individually questioned, and each claimed I had bragged that I had stolen the money.

I stuttered, "I-I-I didn't do it."

He leaned towards me, a stern look on his face. "You know, of course, that if you did steal the money, you are in serious trouble," he said. "In all likelihood, this will go to the police, and then to the courts, where prosecutors will try you as a juvenile offender. You'll certainly be expelled from this school. You'll save yourself a lot of unpleasantness if you cooperate." Washington did not usually talk so bluntly. In retrospect, I imagine he consciously employed a "scared straight" approach to frighten the holy bejesus out of me. If so, mission accomplished.

"But I didn't do it!" I practically shouted.

Mr. Washington leaned back slightly, eyeing me. "Do you remember telling three students at this school that you did?" He might as well have added, "Checkmate."

My shoulders slumped; I looked down at my sneakers and gazed glassy-eyed at my fidgeting feet.

Mr. Washington informed me that he had no choice but to suspend me until authorities resolved the matter. He added that he had called my grandmother, who was on her way to school. When I heard that, I became dizzy. All my blood seemed to rush away from my arms and legs. The world around me began to spin. Some people might think I was soft, that I overreacted. Compared to being accused of mugging, carjacking, dope peddling, or sexual assault, stealing, even from a friend, might seem like small potatoes, even if nobody believed I was innocent. But for as long as I could remember, I had been haunted by a feeling difficult to describe. Even in Oakwood, a town of forty thousand, 30 percent of whom were black. Although we were "integrated" into the community, evenly spread throughout the town's economic spectrum, from Section 8 housing to mansions, I always felt in some way inauthentic. Despite my trophies, report cards, and test scores, I never quite trusted, nor did I feel entirely trusted by my surroundings. I felt a nagging discomfort like an illness that never entirely presents itself but that never entirely goes away. Could that feeling be what Dad meant when he talked about being a black man—or did white men have that feeling, also?

Wood and glass rattled as somebody rapped on the door. Mr. Washington got up and walked three or four steps to open it, revealing Blackmun. He stood still for a long moment, expressionless. His face resembled those I had known from the photographs in the many books of African art Dad had purchased over the years. Specifically, it resembled the West African dance mask Dad had hung with pride on a wall in his home office. A contemporary copy of a famous nineteenth-century mask from the Dan people, it was made of ebony and was flawlessly smooth. As a child, I had sat in Dad's home office in his leather chair many times—elbows on the desk, left hand cradling my jaw and chin, neck crooked slightly to the right in the direction of the mask. I would sit there for hours, lost in the graceful curves of the eyebrows, the lightly parted lips (which seemed to me to be whispering a secret), and the eyes. While I couldn't conceptualize it when I was a child, the eyes—simple rectangular slits—seemed to offer a glimpse into worlds parallel to ours that were full of promise. And for a second in the principal's office, my memory of the mask and Blackmun's face in front of me were one: Black. Steady. Indomitable.

The principal said, "I'll leave so you men can talk," and left the room. Blackmun walked in and shut the door. Now it was just us. Two legs of the other tan chair made a rasping sound as Blackmun grabbed it by the back and briskly dragged it across the floor nearer to me.

"You know, it crossed my mind that you or J.J. might have taken the money," Blackmun said as he sat down, our knees practically touching. "But I dismissed the thought. It just didn't make sense."

"I didn't do it, Blackmun!" I exclaimed.

Blackmun frowned. "Don't you think it's curious that three kids—friends of yours—individually said you claimed you did?" I felt miserable and ashamed. Although I hadn't taken the money, I'd lied and said I did it to impress my friends.

When I confessed this to Blackmun, he slowly shook his head. "Stealing? Is that what your friends find impressive?" he asked wearily. In the silence that followed, I became aware of a thin buzzing, like the sound of a mosquito, but it came from inside my head.

Blackmun took a deep breath. With a mixture of confusion and sorrow, he said, "Let me get this straight, you did this—you *claimed* to do this—not for diapers for a child or food for your family or to keep the lights on, but...but for what?"

I thought about how I was disgracing the memory of my father and mother.

There was another rap at the door, and Grandma swung it wide. Standing in the doorway, she said, "Is this true what I hear, that you have been stealing! And from Blackmun, yet!" Her eyes were on fire. She walked over to where I was sitting and swooped down on me. Though she was midway through her seventh decade, she gripped one of my upper arms with a ferocity that hurt. She was about to pull me to my feet so that she could confront me face-to-face. But I noticed Blackmun caught her eye and made a subtle gesture with his hands, indicating that he and I were in the middle of something.

Grandma released my arm. In a tone more sad than angry, she asked, "Is this true, baby?"

No one talked for at least a full minute. Finally, Blackmun spoke to Grandma. "Look, I don't believe he stole this money." Then he looked at me. "It just isn't like you. But what I don't understand is why you'd *boast* that you were a thief?"

"It was a big deal with J.J.," I explained. "J.J. tried to talk me into stealing the money, but I couldn't do it."

I felt I was done for. I winced as I remembered what Blackmun had told me at the store: *If you run with people like that, be careful of what you do. You and you alone will be held accountable for your actions.*

I was about to ask Blackmun if he would vouch for me and help me get out of this mess when the principal reentered the room. Grandma asked Mr. Washington what the next move would be. I felt lightheaded again. "I'll wait until tomorrow before I call the police...," Mr. Washington began.

"I don't think the police will be necessary," Blackmun interrupted.

The principal responded using excessively formal language, even for him. With the benefit of hindsight, I think he did this less to present a calm and collected argument and more to rein in, or perhaps disguise, the worry that he must have known his face betrayed.

"Blackmun, with all due respect, we must contact the police—the sooner, the better," he said. "Five hundred dollars is no mean sum, and I doubt you'll see it again without the assistance of the law. But I'm mainly concerned about the future of our young man here. Now is the time to check this kind of behavior before it becomes a habit, or worse, a tributary to more serious transgressions. Intervening now could save his life."

Blackmun sat silently for a long time, his eyes downcast in thought. When he raised them, he looked at Mr. Washington and said softly, "How are you doing, Jim?"

The office became unexpectedly quiet—the sounds of birds outside Mr. Washington's window and the murmur of his secretary talking on the phone just beyond the closed door were suddenly vacuumed into silence. The atmosphere became one of melancholy and exhaustion. Underneath the harsh glare of the fluorescent lights, Mr. Washington's eyes locked onto something that seemed light years away. He placed his right index finger pensively to his closed lips and tapped them several times.

"I'm OK, Chuck," he finally replied quietly and with an informality I found disorienting. "But you know, every day is a struggle."

What I didn't know until years later was that Mr. Washington's nephew, Darius, had been tricked into confessing to an offense he didn't commit. One night in the middle of a crime wave in Chicago, police were searching for the perpetrators of a particularly heinous attack. While trawling for young black men, most of whom didn't even fit the description of the assailants, Mr. Washington's nephew got caught in the net when he was innocently hanging out with friends on a street corner. The cops told Darius while he was in custody that he could go home if he said he committed the crime. Darius signed the confession the cops had written for him, then threw him in jail. He was thirteen when he was arrested and fourteen when he was convicted. A couple of high-profile attorneys took up the case, and the family did all they could to free him with their own detective work while trying to sustain media interest in the case over the years— all to no avail. A week before our present conversation in Mr. Washington's office, correctional officers had found Darius dead of an apparent suicide in his cell. He had just turned eighteen years old.

"I see where you're coming from, Jim," Blackmun said compassionately. "Under our protection, a rap on the knuckles now in the form of a brief encounter with the cops might prevent him from really getting hurt later. But getting the police involved unnecessarily may have unintended consequences. It's unpredictable. But the larger issue here is that, despite Miles's uncoerced confession, or rather, his bragging"—Blackmun stopped and gave me a sharp look—"I simply don't believe he did it."

Blackmun turned and spoke sternly: "OK, Miles, you say you are innocent. I believe you. But now, you have to prove it to all of us."

It had never occurred to me that J.J. would steal the money if I didn't. That explained where J.J. had come up with the five-hundred-dollar figure. But I knew he would never confess to the theft. I admit it—I was scared. I had to prove my innocence, and I hadn't the slightest idea how.

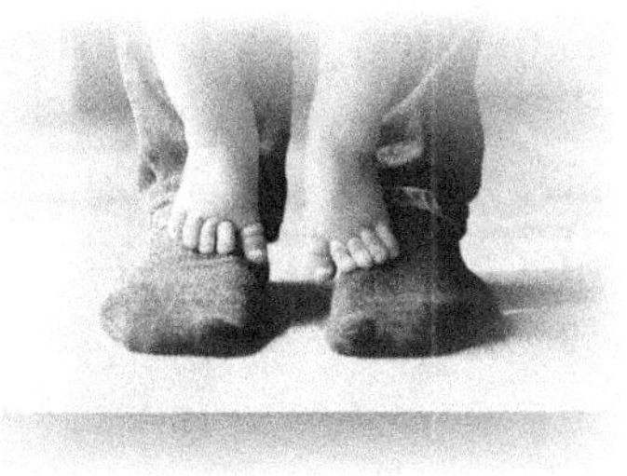

THE
STARRY
NIGHT

That evening, after Grandma had gone to work, I put together a simple green salad: red oak lettuce, fresh oregano, fresh thyme, cherry tomatoes, red onions, apple cider vinaigrette, and a few flakes of coarse sea salt. I microwaved the spicy Texas-style chili Grandma had made for dinner that morning for the twins and me, which we eagerly sopped up with hero-sized slices of cornbread, made with buttermilk and real corn kernels. Grandma had made the cornbread in her heirloom cast-iron skillet. Once the twins finished helping me clean up and put the dishes in the dishwasher, I let them watch *Kenan & Kel*, a television sitcom series about the wacky misadventures of a pair of Chicago high school students that we had recorded on the VCR before it went off the air earlier in the year. At about nine, I checked to see that my brother and sister were washed, then tucked them into bed and made sure to say their special prayers to them.

Once the twins were squared away, I went downstairs and idly channel surfed. I didn't realize it at the time, but I wasn't looking for entertainment, I was trying to create a mental blank slate, hoping that an answer to my predicament might magically appear, like a rabbit popping out of an empty top hat. After a few minutes, I turned off the set, walked around the house, and checked to make sure the front, back, and basement doors were locked, then I headed upstairs to my bedroom. I grabbed the now singed kente cloth Blackmun had given me off the outer doorknob to my bedroom, entered my room, shut the door, and sat at my desk. I casually rubbed the fabric with my forefinger, and as I noted its silky texture, my mind rose from the turbulence of my thoughts. The weight of my body seemed to drift away. I felt myself expanding beyond the boundaries of my skin. I felt myself rising like infinitely fine mist, passing through my ceiling, through the clutter in the attic, through the shingles of the roof, and into the inky vastness of the starry night. Beyond the starry night, I accelerated through soundscapes of sibilant, sighing waves, rumbling desert sand dunes, moaning walls of falling ice, and forests of whispering leaves. As I entered each realm, my entire being shuddered. It was as if someone had swung a sledgehammer and shattered my soul, producing electrifying jolts that reverberated far and wide.

A cloud of red dust flew up around me. Startled and dazed, I lifted my head and wiped my eyes. It was either sunrise or sunset. I had landed on an endless plain of red, sun-cracked clay. I scanned the horizonless distance where land and sky merged in the ochre half-light. I squinted and saw a dark, round object—a speck in the far, far distance. In half the time it takes to draw one breath, the branches of a baobab tree covered me in a jagged web of shadows. The Ashanti king and his entourage of soldiers now were only a few feet away. The king sat on a wooden stool, his legs spread wide, hands relaxed on their corresponding thighs, a study in authority and equilibrium. He was resplendent in the wedges, spires, and arcs that comprised the jewel-like geometry of the folds of his royal robe. Its colors—ruby red, emerald green, sapphire blue, and glittering gold—were so radiant they made my eyes ache as if I were looking directly at the sun. I had to turn away from their brilliance.

He was flanked by a hundred soldiers, distributed evenly on each side. They gazed ahead, expressionless. They wore Union Army uniforms of the American Civil War. Each had a musket resting on his shoulder. The king faced away from me. Then, almost imperceptibly, something mysterious moved my body, so that little by little, the king's serene gaze eventually fell directly on me.

A gentle stream of air, soft as a baby's breath inches from my left ear, surprised me. I caught the scent of something soothing and sweet—some herb or spice, perhaps. The adviser's voice addressed me. Its tone was calm but urgent and located inches from my right ear.

"I will tell you a story. When I finish, I will ask you a question. You may not move from that spot until you answer that question. Your life depends on your answer to that question."

And with that, I heard the clank of metal as the king's soldiers cocked their weapons and pointed them at me.

~

A Black Man guides a half dozen slaves to freedom. At the end of the first day, they make an overnight stop in an empty cabin in a forest. The next morning, when it's time to continue, the former captives refuse to open the cabin door. They are afraid of the wild beasts they heard outside during the night.

But the Black Man tells the group he has made dozens of journeys through these parts. He's traveled under daylight, moonlight, and through moonless darkness. He's slept in cabins, caves, and under the stars in this area. He's traveled in all seasons. He has traveled through rain, sleet, snow, and debilitating heat—through droughts and through floods. He is intimately familiar with the plants and animals in these parts and has foraged for them and hunted them for food.

I've never seen even one wild beast around here, the Black Man said. The nearest wild beasts are miles away.

We have traveled in forests like this before, said one of the former captives. Despite your reassurances, we know there are wild beasts. We know their signs. We've been mauled by them in broad daylight and bear those scars.

If there are no wild beasts in this area, another in the group said, what was that ghostly howling all last night?

The wind passing through the trees, the Black Man answered.

What were those shadows moving at the bottom of the door? asked another.

Deer walking towards the nearby pond to drink, the Black Man replied.

What was the scratching at the back wall of the cabin?

Raccoons searching for food, the Black Man responded.

Yet despite every reasonable explanation, the slaves remained steadfast in their belief that wild beasts were right outside the door, ready to devour them, and they refused to budge. Finally, the fugitives confidently followed the Black Man out of the cabin door towards freedom.

~

The king's adviser looked at me solemnly: How did the Black Man convince the group that there were no beasts in the area?

The sun and stars completed their circuit twenty-one times when an answer streaked like a comet across the wine-colored sky. I reached up and grabbed it; words like red-hot coals leaped from my lips.

"The black man stopped trying to convince the slaves that there were no wild beasts around," I said. "Instead, the black man taught the slaves how to vanquish wild beasts."

The king nodded in agreement. I laughed with relief.

"We have another task for you," the adviser's voice said to me.

I turned around. About thirty-five feet away, the length of a school bus, stood a humanoid figure with its back to me. Stoop-shouldered and motionless, it wore a powder blue tailcoat and scarlet pants. The backs of its black, spit-shined patent leather shoes gleamed just below the cuffs of its pant legs.

The shape sleepily straightened up as it turned in my direction, revealing a corona of wildly unkempt hair and a face caked with coal-colored mud—a kind of crude blackface. The mud had dried and cracked so that a lacy pattern of skin was visible underneath. A chalky white circle ringed each eye and a thick, crimson parody of Negro lips covered its mouth and rose like a gash on either cheek. The collar of its white shirt was obscured by a clownishly large yellow bow tie.

Years later I found out the creature resembled a golliwog—one of many grotesque caricatures devised to denigrate black people. These kinds of images were used prolifically during the Jim Crow era on everyday items—ink bottle labels, ashtrays, saltshakers, and packages for food and tobacco, for instance. In retrospect, I wonder how the image of a golliwog had seeped into my subconscious, since it was only in my college years that I learned about them.

The creature before me cast its gaze about the landscape haphazardly, but when its eyes landed on me, its demeanor changed. It became taut and predatory. I looked at the soldiers, hoping they'd protect me, since I had answered the question. But they had returned their rifles to their shoulder and gazed ahead impassively.

I was choked by anger, frozen with fear. This was unjust, I thought. I had played by the rules. I'd answered the question correctly.

I shouted to no one in particular, "This isn't right. This isn't fair."

"You are correct: it's not right. It's not fair," came the adviser's stern reply.

"But I don't want to die," I said angrily.

"No one wants to die!" the adviser's pitiless voice thundered in response. "Focus!"

I tried to move my legs to run away but couldn't. I felt as if I was standing knee deep in sand. I heard footsteps accelerating in my direction. A paralyzing blow to my stomach jackknifed me, launching my butt cartoonlike several feet into the air, while my arms and legs flew out in front of me. My rear end landed on the ground with a bone-rattling thwack. The golliwog had run into my belly, shoulder first, and sent me flying.

It was now about two dozen yards on the other side of me. It hopped up and down with both feet and pumped the air in elation with its tiny, white-gloved fists, shrieking like a chimpanzee. It stomped—actually, it was more of a victory dance—in a tight circle. It seemed happily isolated in its bubble of delirious fury. I was thankful it seemed to have forgotten about me when suddenly it stopped. It let its right arm fall casually by its side and tightened its grip around the handle of a machete that had materialized in its hand. The weapon's blade glistened menacingly. The creature robotically cocked its head in sharp angles up and down, left and right, as if searching for something. When it finally saw me, its eyes became liquid with anticipation, and it smiled like a child impatient to unwrap a Christmas present.

It charged at me. With each step, its facial expression dissolved from one emotion into another—from happiness to anticipation; from anticipation to determination; from determination to urgency; from urgency to glee. As it ran towards me, it raised the machete high with both hands to multiply the force of the blow it was directing at the top of my skull.

I held up my arms and crossed them at the wrists to defend myself. The blade came down with a swift swish of efficiency clean through my forearms. The golliwog let out an ear-withering squeal of excitement as I felt him deliver two horizontal slashes across my neck, then a blow to my gut as the blade entered my abdomen and tore upward towards my sternum. The pain was excruciating. I saw shards of light as it plunged the blade tip and twisted it into my left eye. But I was uninjured. No matter how savage the attack, no matter how persistent. My body had the quality of water—fluid, regenerative, and resilient.

The golliwog jumped back and walked in a circle around me. It was alert but relaxed, apparently taking its time in planning its next attack.

"Breathe," a voice commanded me. I tentatively inhaled through my nose and exhaled through my mouth. A gale-force roar surprised me when it blasted out of my lungs. Upon the gust's impact, my tormentor stopped in place and whirled ferociously like a top, the color of its clothes—powder blue, yellow, and scarlet—forming horizontal streaks of those colors. As it decelerated and finally stopped spinning, it seemed confused and perturbed for a moment. When it caught sight of me again, it charged in my direction.

"Breathe," the voice repeated. I took another breath and exhaled with more confidence this time. A long eruption of purifying heat exploded out of my lungs, pushing the creature back a good twenty feet. My next deep exhalation shredded the clothes, flayed the skin, and tore the muscles layer by layer off the menace. Finally, the onslaught of the hurricane-force strength of my lungs left only strips of flapping raw flesh and bloody cloth clinging tenuously to the skeleton, which remained standing for a few seconds before collapsing to form a pile of bones.

I took a deep rejuvenating breath, puffed up my chest and slowly turned around, commanding the entire 360 degrees of the landscape. I was ready to take on all comers.

"Anything else?" I shouted, defiantly.

After a beat, a distant voice replied nonchalantly, "Not today...." And I was alone on the vast, bleak plain. Flashes of lightning in the distance illuminated the ghostly silhouette of the baobab tree. A moment later, I heard the welcome rumble of thunder. I stretched my arms heavenward and opened my hands as the first revitalizing drops of rain fell and ran down my cheeks.

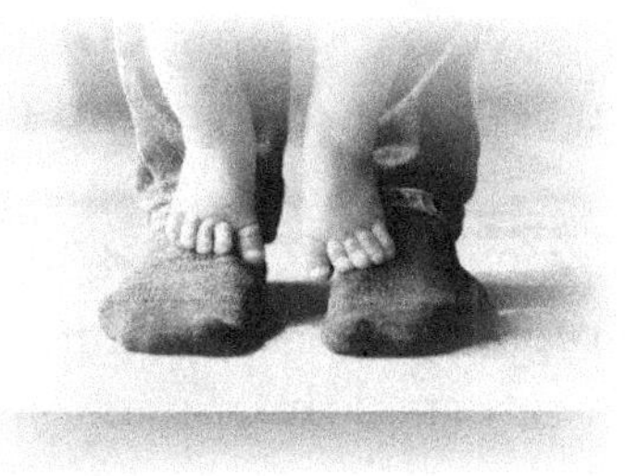

BATTLEFIELDS
AND
BATTLE LINES

I stayed at home for a couple of days to brace myself for the confrontation I knew awaited me when I returned to school. On Friday afternoon, just as sixth-period gym class ended, I walked onto campus towards the gym, the sizzling sound of showers growing louder as I approached the building. As soon as I entered the locker room, the stifling, malodorous humidity smacked me in the face like a dirty wet sock. J.J. was at the far end of the row of blue lockers. He was holding court, joking around with our three friends from the cafeteria earlier in the week. They had just finished getting dressed and seemed like they were about to leave.

When J.J. saw me walking towards the group, he looked startled. But only for an unguarded instant.

"I thought you were suspended," J.J. said evenly.

"I was," I replied, "but Blackmun agreed to drop everything if I returned the money—so I did."

J.J. eyed me leerily. "You gave him back five hundred dollars?!"

"It was either that or get expelled and end up in who knows what kind of mess," I said matter-of-factly.

J.J. rubbed his chin thoughtfully. He seemed to have trouble putting this together. Other than that weird incident with the photograph at the Corner Store, it was the only time J.J. seemed genuinely flustered, at a loss for words. "Why'd you leave money behind?" J.J. finally asked.

"What are you talking about?" I said, narrowing my eyes to emphasize my question. "Like I said, I saw the money—and I took it."

J.J. thought for a moment, then chuckled softly. "No, there was still five hundred left when I snuck in." He dug his right hand into his inside jacket pocket and came out with a wad of folded bills, presumably a portion of his take. He waved the cash in the air, taunting me with it.

"What?" I asked, trying my best to look simultaneously surprised, angry, and disappointed.

"You must have been nervous or mixed up envelopes or something because there was still five hundred bucks in that drawer when I got there. Too bad you got caught."

The three friends looked at J.J. in disbelief. When I had phoned them individually the previous evening and told them J.J. had stolen the money, they thought I was lying. They thought I was desperately and pathetically trying to get off the hook. One of them had ragged on me mercilessly for trying to blame someone else for the theft I had bragged about. They were all especially disappointed that I should try to blame it on a good friend. But when I told them they could witness J.J.'s confession from his own lips, curiosity got the better of them. They knew I would show up in the locker room after their sixth-period gym class, and they knew they would witness someone's moment of truth—either mine or J.J.'s.

Now all of us stood in the narrow aisle of lockers looking at one another, speechless. Finally, the heavyset teen with reddish hair addressed J.J.

"Yo, that's messed up, J.J.," he said, a trace of uncertainty in his voice.

"What's messed up?" J.J. shot back, his voice dripping with intimidation.

"Letting Miles take the rap for what you did," asserted the tall boy.

Neither of them would have challenged J.J. individually, but together they seemed to find the courage to do it.

"OK," J.J. said after a pause. "I took some of Blackmun's money, but so did Miles. He bragged about it, and he got caught."

"I never stole any money," I told J.J. "Blackmun only had five hundred dollars in the drawer, and he will testify to that.”

"And you showed us the money," the tall boy said to J.J.

Another long period of silence followed.

"So, what are you going to do, J.J.?" the heavy-set boy asked at last, a hint of hesitancy having crept into his voice.

When J.J. didn't answer, the tall boy suggested half-heartedly, "Maybe you should go tell Blackmun and Washington the truth."

"Or perhaps you want us to do it," the boy with the shaved head said tenuously.

I could see that J.J. had begun reasserting his dominance over our friends. He glared at the other three and they looked away from him. Then he looked at me. I could see J.J. grinding his jaw muscles. My eyes panned down to his hands. I'd learned from watching television shows to check your opponent's hands to see if he had a ring on his finger or was clutching a set of keys, to inflict maximum damage with each punch. J.J.'s hands were empty, but he was inconspicuously balling them into steely fists. He leveled his eyes at me. I remembered J.J.'s boasts of "having served" a few guys in his old neighborhoods. I remembered the incident with the guard at the mall. Perhaps I was about to find out if J.J. was as good as his boasts.

My heart raced, and I felt my feet go cold. This was real life. Based on my friends' tepid defense of me about the crime, I didn't feel I could count on them to bust up or referee if J.J. and I mixed it up. My breathing became shallow. I was on my own. I became light-headed. I could feel my blood tingling just under my skin and surging throughout my entire body. I hoped he couldn't see that my lips quivered in fear. It wasn't a fair match. He was noticeably bigger than me and an unexpected quick punch on his part would surely send me reeling back onto the metal lockers. It might knock me unconscious. I suddenly had an overwhelming urge to pee. Maybe I should throw the first punch.

Then a strange serenity descended over me. My belly began rising and falling with waves of expanding breaths. My heart slowed down. My feet warmed to a comforting heat that seemed to come from the center of my being. All the while, through my fear, readiness, and serenity, I had continued looking at J.J. I never broke my gaze—not once. I never flinched.

Finally, J.J. erupted, in answer to whether he'd confess to Blackmun, "I'll think about it," and stormed out of the locker room. Alone.

Several weeks went by, and I had seen neither hide nor hair of J.J. at school. Clearly, he'd come clean to Blackmun, and they had reached some sort of agreement, but I was vaguely curious about the details. I had considered asking our pals whether any of them had talked to J.J., but the question would have reminded them of a very ugly predicament I was eager to put behind me. I made sure not to ask Blackmun the few times I saw him after the incident, and he behaved as if nothing had happened. I even considered calling J.J. himself to get a status report but thought better of it. At best, he'd think I was looking for his approval or regretted my actions in some way; at worst, that I wanted to gloat. So, questions about J.J.'s whereabouts, mood, or arrangements with Blackmun remained unanswered.

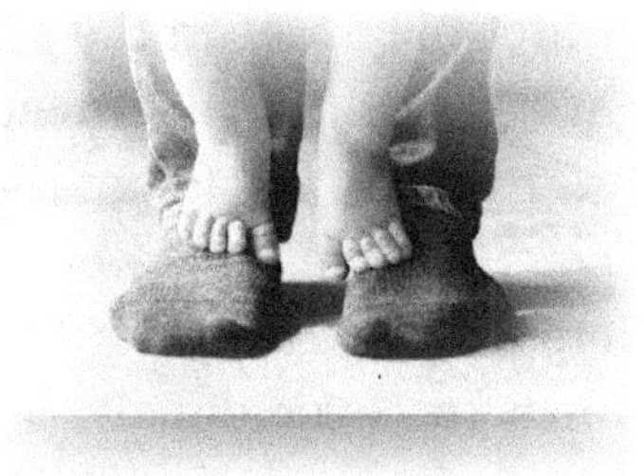

HOMECOMING

On a day when temperatures invited frostbite in minutes on bare skin, the twins and I sat in Grandma's red Toyota Camry. Grandma was at the wheel. We'd just passed the packed parking lot of our church, our destination, and now searched for a spot as close to it as possible. We considered ourselves lucky to find one only a couple of blocks away. Grandma expertly parallel parked between a blue minivan and a hillock of fresh snow. The day before, a blizzard had blanketed our area with over a foot of snow, but our county's crack road crews had almost immediately cleared our town's streets.

Temperatures hadn't risen above freezing for over a week, but it was New Year's Eve 2000—the beginning of a new century and a new millennium. How often does that happen? So Grandma decided we should brave the elements to experience this once-in-a-lifetime event in the actual physical presence of our community. She turned off the engine, and the soft whir of the fan of the car's heater faded to silence. She, the twins, and I pulled our woolen mufflers up to our noses, and our woolen watch caps down to cover our eyebrows. Finally, we zipped up our coats, donned our mittens, and, opening the car doors, tumbled out into the bracing night air.

We trudged over the icy sidewalks, enduring occasional sharp gusts of wind that bit into the few exposed parts of our faces. As we made our way, ten, fifty, two hundred, eventually innumerable black people converged towards the church with us. They came from every terrestrial direction: north, northeast, east, southeast, south, south-southwest...and from above, also. They drifted slowly from the sky like paratroopers landing with a nimble running step. The quick, soft, crunching patter of their feet decelerated to a leisurely gait as they touched down on the iced-over snow. All of us headed towards the gray, rough-hewn stone bell tower of the hundred-year-old church our congregation had purchased from another congregation during the civil rights era. The crowd narrowed into a single shivering stream moving in the general direction of the church doors. A large electric sign sat on the lawn to the right of the concrete walkway heading to the church steps. Ordinarily emblazoned with weekly affirmations or meditations from prominent black people, on this frigid night, the sign offered Harriet Tubman's famous quote, "I freed thousands of slaves. I could have freed thousands more if they had known they were slaves."

The crowd funneled towards the building's pair of colossal black lacquered doors that led to the covered porch. Four distinguished-looking black men, who seemed to range in age from their midtwenties to midsixties, flanked the entrance to the church proper. Instead of the dark two-piece suit, dark tie, white shirt, and white gloves our church ushers usually wore, these men sported dark, brass-buttoned three-piece suits for tonight's special service. Embroidered in gold thread on the left breast pocket of the coats: "Underground RR." A dark, brimmed hat bearing a narrow chrome nameplate reading "Conductor" crowned each of their heads. The caps also had a much larger metal plate, each etched with a different number—1619, 1863, 1964, 1494. The ushers each held a pocket watch attached to a watch fob.

Grandma rummaged in her purse for our tickets as we approached the men. She handed me mine while retaining those for her and the twins. She nudged me to look at my ticket, then talked to the twins about theirs. The tickets were about as firm as an index card and about the size and shape of a dollar bill. One side read "boarding pass," illustrated with broken chains turning into airborne birds with the dates Dec. 31, 2000/Jan. 1, 2001; the other side included a brief paragraph about an event or person from the history of the African diaspora. Mine read: *1955 — Rosa Parks ignites the yearlong Montgomery, Alabama bus boycott when she re-*

fuses to give up her seat for a white passenger. It launched the modern-day civil rights movement. The local NAACP had been planning this action for years.

As we inched towards the door, I noticed that the ushers looked at the adults' tickets, then at their watches, and then at the adult, and said with a huge smile, "You're right on time!" or "We've been expecting you!" before punching the ticket. The ushers chatted briefly with the younger audience members as they entered.

When Ida and Douglass reached the front of the line, one of the two middle-aged ushers, who wore the 1494 hat, knelt so that his face met theirs.

"Well, young man, what do you want to be when you grow up?" he asked.

"I want to play shooting guard on the Chicago Bulls like Michael Jordan," Douglass replied without hesitation.

"Play with the team? I bet you can own the team!" the usher replied with equal gusto.

In her small but firm voice, Ida responded thoughtfully, "I want to be an artist, like Faith Ringgold."

The usher replied, "It's a blessing to heal this world with beauty."

The eldest usher, who had become a congregant only recently, locked eyes with Grandma when taking the ticket from her hand. It sounds weird to say, but he seemed to punch her ticket sensuously— meaning S-L-O-W-L-Y, and he held it a shade longer than necessary when returning it to her hand.

"You're right on time, Sistuh," he said, his voice oozing across each syllable like butter melting on a hot biscuit. She giggled softly like a schoolgirl. The twins seemed to sense something was going on, but they weren't sure what exactly. They tugged at her jacket, pulling her towards the pews, but her eyes lingered on the usher until the twins towed her deeper into the church.

When I gave one of the other conductors, the youngest one, my ticket, he looked at me, punched the ticket, and simply said, "Welcome," before turning his attention to the person behind me.

I crossed over the inner doorway of the church and glimpsed something to my far left. I turned my head and saw a group of five young women rising at a thirty-degree angle in thin air. Their clothes featured the colors salmon pink and apple green. They chatted among themselves nonchalantly as if floating upwards was normal, like riding an ascending escalator. As I gazed at them, I heard a rustling sound behind me. I turned around and saw what I took to be a family—mother, father, and two teenaged boys around my age. They were taking off their coats, gloves, and mufflers. Oddly, their clothes seemed decades out of fashion— like something I'd seen black people wearing in sepia-tinted photographs of the Great Migration. I watched the family lift off the floor, their feet dangling in the air as they rose towards the ceiling, when my attention was diverted by a familiar voice.

"Watcha readin', fam!" said Blackmun, walking towards us from one side of the church. He looked dapper in his black slacks and black turtleneck shirt, offset with a kente cloth–inspired vest of red, blue, and gold. A matching kente cloth stole draped his neck.

"Books on love," Grandma said wistfully, stealing a glance at the elder usher who happened to take an approving sneak peek at Grandma as he punched another ticket at the doorway.

"I heard that!" said Blackmun, winking.

"You know, I never found out what happened to J.J.," Grandma said as she bent down to help my siblings take off their coats. "Miles tells me he hasn't been at school. Has he been expelled?"

"Not at all," Blackmun said. "Everyone—his parents, the principal, his teachers, me, and even J.J. himself thought school might be a little too hectic for him right now. He'll return in the new semester, at the beginning of the year. In the meantime, he's been keeping up with his studies at home.

"J.J. owned up to what he did; I told him to return my money, and he did, except for the sixty dollars he'd spent," Blackmun said. "J.J., his parents, and I agreed that he would work on my rental property each day of Christmas break and one day every weekend until Reverend Adams and I launch our rite of passage program for young men, and J.J. will be obliged to participate in it."

Douglass's eyes widened.

"That sounds like a *big* punishment, Blackmun," he said. "I thought you got back most of your money."

Blackmun bent down so that he was looking at Douglass eye-to-eye. "It's *not* a punishment," Blackmun said deliberately but kindly. "And it's *not* about money. It's about faith. Some of our young men, no matter where or how they grow up, confuse being a thug with being a warrior." Blackmun stood up. "You know the difference, don't you, Miles."

I was caught off guard. First, I couldn't tell by his inflection whether he was posing a question, issuing a statement, or making an accusation. Second, I wasn't expecting an Afro "pop" quiz a few hours before an event that hadn't happened in a thousand years. But mainly, I felt a reflexive panic at not knowing how to respond appropriately.

Douglass interrupted: "You even have faith in J.J.?" he asked.

"Yes, even J.J.," Blackmun said. "I was well into adulthood before I learned the difference between thugs and warriors," he said, laughing. "But our community never gave up on me, and I'm not giving up on J.J. All black people, especially young black men and women, are our future. And I'm not about to give up on our future."

"We should head to our neighbors over there who are saving a seat for us," Grandma said, pointing to a woman standing and waving at us from the middle pew on the right.

"And I've got to change clothes to give my part of the presentation," said Blackmun, and he turned to walk towards the altar.

I followed Grandma and my siblings through the crowd toward our neighbors. I had taken a few steps when I began to laugh. I laughed and laughed and laughed. Although I could barely catch my breath, I couldn't stop laughing.

Grandma turned to me, with a concerned look in her eyes, and asked, "Miles, are you alright, pumpkin?"

"It's so obvious, Grandma," I told her. "Hold on."

I spun around and called out to Blackmun several times as I pushed through the crowd towards him. He looked coolly in my direction.

"Blackmun," I repeated when I reached him. "The difference between a thug and a warrior is this: a thug attacks his community; a warrior defends it."

Blackmun made an ambiguous movement with his chin; the look in his eyes was noncommittal. After a long moment of silence infused with anticipation, he smiled slowly and said, "Welcome, Black Man. We've been expecting you."

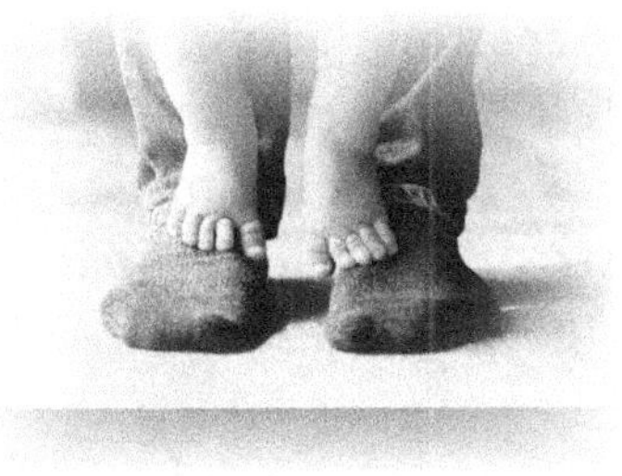

THE TALK

Blackmun began his presentation by explaining Kwanzaa, the African-American cultural holiday celebrated from December 26 to January 1. He described its origins, traditions, symbols, meaning, and variations around the U.S. and worldwide.

He then gave a stirring speech which the congregation punctuated with shouts of "amen," "preach, brotha," and "yes, yes! yes!" He talked about how African-Americans, in particular, are beginning what he called "our third migration."

"The first migration was a forced migration—the slave trade over the turbulent waves of the Atlantic Ocean," he said. "The second began in the early twentieth century—the Great Migration, when black families fled the poverty and violence of the southern states. Those families rode on trains past the heartland's amber waves of grain to the promised land of Chicago, Detroit, New York, and other northern cities.

"Our latest migration is our Greatest Migration, and our greatest challenge, so far," he said somberly. "This time we're heading towards the future on our brain waves—the stories we tell ourselves about who we are, the priorities we set for ourselves as a people...

"This includes understanding that black people, wherever we are or have been, share the same goals—economic, political, and social empowerment. The rub comes when deciding how best to accomplish those goals. But we should applaud the diversity of our perspectives. Think about it as us being on the same sports team. We play different positions, but we have the same goal in mind. And what kind of team would it be that put all their players in one position? Imagine a baseball team in which all nine players clustered at shortstop, or a football team where everybody played center. Shucks, over the years, I've gone through my own phases—from fierce integrationist to fierce segregationist, from black nationalist to black assimilationist, and everything in between and back again. Not to say we should make frivolous or ill-considered changes, but thoughtful re-evaluation of approaches makes sense. I've been around for a long, long, long time and noticed that different eras and different places and different circumstances demand different strategies; it's important to be alert to that.

"Black Christians, black Moslems, black Jews, and black Buddhists, the followers of the old gods of our motherland, and those who believe in no god all travel together on our latest, greatest journey.

Black Democrats and black Republicans, black Marxists, and black capitalists, also. We may fuss with one another every so often—some say too often—and get frustrated with some of us who seem to pull up the rear. But our most enlightened community members realize we're all on the same side. To switch metaphors, our progress is not about finding "the key," it's about finding the right combination to unlock economic, political, and social power at any given moment in history, as long as we don't take our frustrations out on one another. Remember, Booker T. Washington and W. E. B. DuBois were contemporaries. So were Malcolm X and Martin Luther King, Jr. ...

Let's celebrate the resilience, strength, and grit that has resulted in the advancement we've made so far. Let's do that by paying homage to our past, which goes back eons before the slave trade. On the count of three, I want you to stand up. I want you to take a moment now to think of at least one black person who has influenced you or meant something to you but who has departed from this world. One. Two. Three..."

As the packed church rose to its collective feet, I heard fluttering all around me, like the flapping wings of hundreds of birds. I assumed the sound came from heavy garments swooshing from the laps of congregants as they deposited their winter-wear on the wooden pews.

I was overcome by an unexpected surge of warmth as I looked around the church. I saw my late father's friends, Grandma's friends, my brother's and sister's friends, and their parents, and my friends and their parents, and teachers and neighbors, too—while Blackmun, resplendent in the folds and geometry of his most regal African robe, presided from the pulpit. I felt surrounded by love—the love of my family, the love of my friends, and the love of my community. I felt as if I was returning to the welcoming caress of home. I embraced the moment—the scores of bodies and minds pulsating with the souls of black folk everywhere and throughout all time.

My spirit visited random people in the packed church as they began giving thanks in their unique way. To my left, a man the color of a brown paper bag stood with his forearms in front of him, his palms open and facing upward, as if he were preparing to catch or cradle something. He angled his head upward, closed his eyes, and thanked Marcus Garvey, Mary McLeod Bethune, Oscar Micheaux, Ella Baker, and a host of other black historical figures for "sharing the road maps that help guide us."

To my right, a mother stood between her daughters, her arms outstretched, resting protectively on their shoulders. Unlike some of the other guests, they wore nothing that was overtly Afrocentric. However, as they bowed their head, I noticed each of them wore cowrie earrings, which hung discreetly from their pierced earlobes. The mother acknowledged John Coltrane and Romare Bearden, and the daughters Tupac Shakur and Jean-Michel Basquiat for bringing "so much truth into our lives."

Shouts and murmurs of thanksgiving rose and fell like waves lapping against a rocky shore, as the lips of person after person formed the names of famous black people and loved ones who had passed away.

As I bowed my head, I clasped my hands together prayerfully in front of my chest and closed my eyes. I found myself mouthing the words "Mom" and "Dad." I barely emitted a sound at first, but as I repeated their names, my voice became passionate in recalling my memory of them, and I found myself fervently thanking them for giving me life and guidance. I repeated my prayer of appreciation to my parents over and over and over again, like a mantra, like a chant, like an incantation, as my hands shot up, palms open as if they had a mind of their own.

Officials in parks throughout the surrounding towns set off fireworks to celebrate the arrival of the new year, the new century, and the new millennium. The muffled pop, crackle, and pow of explosions seeped through the church walls, but none of the congregants noticed, or at least they seemed to pay it no mind.

I lifted my head expecting to see the familiar cream-colored plaster ceiling of the church, but instead my eyes greeted a swirling vault that oscillated between indigo and electric blue. This inverted vortex spiraled infinitely upward and filled me with a boundless sense of awe. Clouds resembling cotton bolls bathed in golden light shimmered in the growing, twirling cone.

Black people of all ages and genders revealed themselves in the vault. They dipped, cartwheeled, and somersaulted in the widening enchantment of the inverted whirlpool. Some wore their hair in a lion's mane Afro. Others kept their hair in dreadlocks, twists, or braids of various kinds. Still others chemically straightened their hair. And some wore wigs. Some wore the armor of the Western business suit; others the relaxed look of sweatshirts and track pants, and still others wore traditional African garb, with its lively colors and flowing curves and turns. A kaleidoscope of black miracles in every shade filled the firmament—chocolate, ebony, tan, chestnut, sepia, café au lait, and everything in between.

Our church members began rising into the ever-growing vault—some ascended swiftly like bubbles in a carbonated drink, others struggled. In the pew in front of me, a family of five—a woman and her two preteen girls and two preteen boys simultaneously bent their knees and launched into the air. They stretched out their arms like jet wings and flew in a V formation, led by the woman, and joined flocks of other families soaring inside the uppermost regions of the vault.

I turned around and looked behind me. Two pews back sat an older man wearing a gray wool herringbone jacket. He stood and turned his expectant face upward. His expression turned to one of frustration and finally yearning as he failed to hover more than a few inches off the floor, even then remaining airborne only in fits and starts. He'd rise two inches or so before falling back an inch, then he'd rise one inch and return to the floor. He failed to take flight, or for that matter, to remain floating more than a foot off the ground for more than a few seconds, no matter how aggressively he jumped, tugged at the air, or flapped his arms.

I looked up to my right and noticed a young man and woman bobbing like helium-filled birthday balloons against a side of the lower part of the dome. They each held one hand of a girl who was perhaps three years old. She wore polka dot peach-and-black socks, a black skirt, and peach and polka dot shirt. When the adults let go of the toddler's hands, she jetted around the dome in delightful corkscrew patterns then returned to the young couple, who laughed and applauded the toddler's flight.

I spied an older woman in the lower part of the dome across from the young couple. She wore a raspberry-red church hat whose wide undulating brim was trimmed with a plum-colored ribbon. The crown of her hat was decorated with a profusion of flame-colored feathers. Her matching wool pants and jacket echoed the colors of her hat—red, with purple satin lapels on the jacket. She didn't flap her arms like a bird, nor did she extend them and keep them in place like a jet or an airplane. Her flying technique consisted of doing a breaststroke—she propelled herself through the air, sweeping her arms forward and back while her knees came in and around frog-style. I was entranced by the blissful expression on her face before I was interrupted by a loud swoosh that passed near me on my right side. I looked up to see what it was. The older man who wore the gray jacket had just rippled past me. He was happily ping-ponging amongst the clouds in a superhero flying posture—one arm outstretched, the other straight by his side. His gray coat had become an iridescent black cape that flapped like a flag in a stiff wind behind him.

The church reverberated with the jubilance of the flight, dance, and laughter of black people from the four corners of the world, from everywhere people of African descent live or have lived. It was a celebration of the power and joy of being black.

Something or someone tapped me behind my right shoulder. I turned and saw Freedom Sommers floating horizontally in the air. She smiled at me and waved hello. There was no trace of the chilliness she'd displayed towards me during our introduction at the Corner Store. She beckoned me with her hand to follow her. I rose effortlessly into the air and we made a couple of unhurried laps side by side around the edge of the deepening dome. Freedom and I made our rounds in leisurely silence. The days and weeks and this very evening had taken their toll on me. My mind, body, and spirit were exhausted, and she seemed to intuit that. Without preamble, she waved goodbye and drifted up and away from me, and eventually disappeared into the pinpoint center of the rising, gently twisting blue funnel. I remained hovering in the air as clouds gathered around me, supporting my legs, embracing my shoulders, and providing a dark, velvety pillow for my head. They lifted me beyond the confines of the church walls, past the twinkling holiday lights decorating Oakwood homes, over the town's snow-covered suburban lawns, through the towering maple trees festooned with icicles, and finally dropped me off at my front door, decorated with our homemade holiday wreath of holly berries, fir branches, and pine cones.

I passed by the living room, which was still suffused with the holiday scent of our Norway spruce Christmas tree. On the mantle over the fireplace sat some symbols of our Kwanzaa celebration: the straw mat, the seven-branched Kwanzaa candelabra—our *kinara*, with its red, green, and black candles—our wood Unity Cup, and ears of dried corn.

I continued moving through the house, drifting up to the second floor. As I floated past the twins' open door, I could see they were fast asleep, yet Grandma was finishing up reciting their special prayers to them. I wafted into my room, changed into my pajamas, and sat on the bed. I reflected on the past year, the past season, and the events of the day. It was the early morning of January 1, 2001, the beginning of a new century, the beginning of our next thousand years. And to kick them both off in the United States—a new president, George W. Bush.

I had recently celebrated my fourteenth birthday and had weathered the first semester of high school. I had lost my father, yet I often felt his presence next to me, whispering in my ear.

I'd turned off my nightstand lamp and crawled into bed when I noticed something—a shadow in the shape of a human figure—dart across the room.

My heart felt as if it would burst out of my chest. I quickly sat up and scanned my room for the intruder. I quietly opened my nightstand drawer and pulled out a flashlight the size and circumference of my forearm that I kept there in case of electrical outages. Holding the flashlight like a club, I stealthily got out of bed and made my way to the closet, whose door was open a crack. I slowly put my left hand around the doorknob then flung the door wide, my right hand raised, ready to pound the heck out of anything that might be hiding in there. Nothing jumped out at me. I closed the closet door, making sure it clicked shut, and returned to bed. But I tucked the flashlight by my side under the covers, just in case.

As I lay on my belly and pulled the covers over my shoulders, random thoughts crossed my mind. Unexpectedly, I wondered what had happened to that frayed, stained strip of kente cloth Blackmun had given me. I seemed to remember the twins last had it. Oh, well, never mind. I would ask them about it tomorrow, in the new year. But as I turned on my back to readjust my covers, I noticed something—a faint glow at the foot of my bed. I sat up. The kente cloth. I grabbed it and examined it in the palm of my open hand. To my surprise, it was no longer frayed, singed, stained, or tattered. It looked as if it had been woven anew. The eerily vivid colors blazed. The cloth's jewel-like splendor blossomed towards me—a glittering sphere of light that became so unbearably bright that my eyes ached as if I were gazing directly at the sun. But I couldn't turn away from it. I closed my eyes and was transported to a dreamscape of radiant darkness. I was its center. Waves of heat pulsated in concentric circles from my belly. Lengthy shadows coiled out from every pore of my body enveloping me slowly in a wooly, ever-expanding cloud of comfort, familiarity, and safety. I opened my eyes; it was as if I had suddenly raised a curtain. The dazzling incandescence of the cloth and my profound blackness had merged. The dazzling incandescence of the cloth and my profound blackness had become one.

BETWEEN
FATHERS
AND
SONS

Questions
for Discussion

1. How does Miles's relationship with his father change at the beginning of the book? Why does the father begin cracking down on Miles and lecturing him all the time?

2. Why does Blackmun take it upon himself to look out for Miles? Is it simply because he was friends with Miles's father, or is there something more to it?

3. What does Blackmun mean when he tells Miles, "I wasn't always a black man."

4. What does J.J. think it means to be a black man? How is this different from Blackmun's opinion on the subject?

5. Why does Miles lie to J.J. and the other boys about stealing Blackmun's money? Was it OK for Miles to lie in this situation, or was it just as bad as if he had actually taken the money?

6. How does the black man persuade the enslaved men to leave the forest cabin in the morning? Why was his approach successful?

7. What does Blackmun mean when he tells Miles, "A warrior defends his community."

8. Why does Blackmun try to "jog" Miles's memory about what it means to be black? Why doesn't Blackmun just tell Miles?

9. How has Miles changed by the end of the book? Will his new attitude last?

ALSO BY ERIC V. COPAGE

Fruits of the Harvest:
Recipes to Celebrate Kwanzaa
and Other Holidays

Soul Food: Inspirational Stories
for African Americans

Black Pearls Book of Love

Black Pearls for Parents

Black Pearls Journal

Black Pearls